AF132079

Best Regards from London

© 2020, Marc Thirot
Édition : BoD – Books on Demand,
12/14 , rond-point des Champs-Élysées, 75008 Paris
Impression : BoD – Books on Demand, Norderstedt, Allemagne

ISBN 978-2-3222215-1-6

Dépôt legal : mai 2020

Adresse de l'auteur :
mtlondon2017@gmail.com

MARC THIROT

Best Regards from London

Contents

THE LETTER

Sydney, November 4th

Dear Elizabeth,

At last I'm coming back to you. After these two long years at the far end of the world, I'm looking forward to kissing you again. Within a couple of months I'll be in London. We will marry as soon as possible.

I love you,

George

When Elizabeth opened the letter from Australia, mailed three weeks before, she was wondering who that George who had sent it could be. She was even more surprised by its content. The name on the envelope was hers, the address was right although there was no number: Elizabeth Jones, Jubilee Street E1, London.

She was living at number 46, and the street was quite long. She did not know anyone who was likely to have spent two years in a country far away from England. She had no lover. It clearly appeared in her mind that another Elizabeth Jones was living in the same street; the postman had obviously been mistaken. So she decided to go to the post office. She was badly welcome by an employee who hardly greeted her when she entered. She gave the letter back and apologized for opening it, even if it was not her fault. The man strangely stared at her while she was asking him if she had a homonym in Jubilee Street. Without answering, he went to the next room where he stayed at least five minutes. When he came back he nodded negatively.

"It's impossible', she said. 'There must be another Elizabeth Jones in Jubilee Street."

The man repeated his 'no' nod. He did not utter a word, and stared at her again. 'Leave me alone', his eyes seemed to say.

Back home, she decided she had only one solution left. She would go down the street, look at the names on the doors, knock if there was to be no name at all, then she would find out which number Elizabeth Jones number two was living at. This took her part of the afternoon. She had to knock at a dozen doors; six persons did not answer, so she took another chance in the evening. She met five of them. There was nobody at number 64. For a few days she went back to the house whose green door never opened. She asked the neighbours about its occupants. The couple at number 63 had moved in a month before and knew absolutely nothing. At number 65 the old man she met was stone deaf, so that she did not learn anything from him either. Yet, after a week of unsuccessful attempts, a woman beggar who was passing by stopped and began to speak to her.

"There is nobody here!"

"There must have been someone!" Elizabeth answered.

"There used to be."

"Tell me, please. Was there a young woman called Elizabeth Jones who was living here?"

"I never knew her surname, but I can tell you her first name is Liz."

"Elizabeth Jones! She couldn't be but Elizabeth Jones!"

The woman looked at her surprisingly.

"I <u>am</u> Elizabeth Jones too. We are homonyms!"

"Oh, gosh!"

"What do you know about her? Please tell me!"

"Why is it so important for you? This is not a nice story anyway. You'd better forget about her."

Elizabeth then told her about the letter she had received. The woman suddenly looked worried.

"Alright, young lady. In this case I must tell you what happened here. A long story, you know."

Come to my house, please. I'll prepare a nice cup of tea with some biscuits, and you will tell me.'

"That sounds fair. Let's go then."

It was about 5 o'clock in the afternoon. It had been a nice day but now it was getting cold, as supposed to be in February.

Once sitting in the lounge the woman had a few biscuits, emptied a cup of tea, then she spoke again.

"Before I start telling you about the whole stuff... My name is Shirley. I was born in the area, in Jamaica Street and I used to live there until two years ago, when my husband died. Without him I couldn't stand living in my house any more; so I found some tenants and I left. Now I live on the streets; that's my choice. Do you know 'The Streets of London'? The song!"

"Oh yes, I must have heard it."

Shirley started singing.

"Have you seen the old man
In the closed-down market
Kicking up the paper,
With his worn out shoes?"

She stopped and stared at Elizabeth.

"You don't remember it, do you?"

"Well, I know the tune..."

"... In his eyes you see no pride
And held loosely at his side
Yesterday's paper telling yesterday's news..."

"... But I don't know the words."

"Never mind, you will learn them later. Let's get back to the point. Well..."

"A long story, you told me..."

"It surely is!"

"And you said 'he called her Liz'!"

"Ah, quite a couple they were. He must have been, let's say, twenty-five ; a skinny young man, not very tall, with a piercing gaze. He looked lively when he was smiling. When he wasn't, he sort of had a haunted look. When they settled in Jubilee Street, my husband was still alive though not feeling so well. I used to come around quite often, just for a walk, and one day I met them by chance. I spoke to them several times; Liz seemed to be quite talkative, which seemed to upset George... I can't believe he wrote this letter... That can't be!"

"Why?"

"Let me tell you, young lady! Sometimes, when she started speaking about herself, he interfered, then he took her by the arm and said they had to go home. I could feel they were a strange couple, until..."

She looked at Elizabeth intensely, then she sighed.

"Until..."

"Well, I was just thinking... you look quite like her; hazel-haired, quite tall and slim. She used to get dressed in a smart way, just like you. You remind me of her."

"Where is she now?"

"Well, dear. Nobody has seen her since that day... That bloody day! As far as I know, she may be in Belgium."

Elizabeth was more and more eager to hear the whole story.

"A few weeks had passed. My husband had died in the meantime. As I couldn't stand staying alone, I got into the habit of going out until I found some tenants. I actually was out most of the time, night and day. One evening, as I was coming near number 64, I heard them shout. 'Leave me alone', I heard her say, 'please don't'. 'Come here at once', he replied, 'or your worst nightmares will come true'. She suddenly cried out in pain; no doubt he was hitting her. Then they were silent again. I remained sitting opposite the street almost all night long. Nothing else happened, but I felt she was having an awful time with him. The next day, I went back there, hoping to see her. I wanted to speak to her. So I knocked at the door of the house. I waited, then I knocked again. After a while, Liz opened. 'Hello', she said, 'I can't let you in. He wouldn't like it if he knew.' 'Come and have a walk with me', I answered. 'All right, I'm coming', she said. At first glance, her face showed no sign of having been beaten. Later, in the street, I noticed a bruise on her right cheek. She had hidden it with some heavy make-up. 'I heard you last night', I said. 'I know; you're often under the porch opposite the street, aren't you?' She told me he was getting more and more violent. He was drunk the night before; he wanted to have sex. Of course she had refused, then he had knocked her out and abused her sexually. It wasn't the first time he had done it."

"Why didn't she leave him?"

"She was kind of bewitched. She lived under the spell of that guy who had been so nice at the beginning, she said. He had been like an angel before turning into a devil. We had a short walk that morning for she had no right to go out, or let anybody into the house. 'He would lock me up if he saw us together', she said. She thanked me for visiting her before we parted. After that day, I came back every evening by nightfall. He beat her every three or four nights; once he became absolutely furious after she had refused to have sex. 'I'm fed up with being raped', she yelled. 'I'm not raping you, you're my girlfriend. I can screw you as much as I want', he shouted back. I must tell you we had short secret meetings about twice a week. In fact, we were to meet the next day, but she didn't come. I waited for an hour then I made up my mind on visiting her. She looked awful; she had a lame left leg and her back hurt. He had whipped her with his belt. 'You must tell the police', I said, 'before he kills you.' I tried to persuade her, but she stubbornly refused."

"You could have been to the police station alone."

"I was tempted, but I thought I couldn't act against her will, and it could have made things worse."

"What happened then?"

"Two weeks passed. They had a few arguments, but he didn't beat her again. Did he feel bad about treating her so brutally? He definitely didn't; he was more devilish than one might believe he could be; he was only waiting until she had recovered. Then, one evening, he aggressed her before going out with something in mind. As soon as he had left, I went to see her to make sure she was fine. He had satisfied himself with giving her 'a smack in the gob', as he said. So I left the house and waited under the little porch as usual, sheltered from the cold and the passers-by. I soon fell asleep."

"Do you still sleep there?"

"No. I haven't slept there since she left."

"Did he come back that night?"

"He actually did. He came back by... three o'clock, but he wasn't alone. Three other guys, as drunk as he was, were singing with him in the street. They entered the house. I was suddenly seized with panic as I imagined what could happen to Liz. I didn't hear anybody shout, but I could see a light in their room, and I knew something was going on. I got up and reached the nearest phone box to call the cops. I told them a young lady was being raped by four drunkards. They didn't take me seriously, so I pushed the matter. I told them that George beat Liz regularly, that he had hurt her badly quite recently. They finally came, about two hours later. The light in the bedroom was off then. George opened the door and let the cops in. I learnt from Liz he had claimed he and his friends were having a drink while talking, and she was quietly asleep. She was too frightened to move; they didn't even go upstairs to check whether he had told them the truth. They just said that a lunatic passer-by had called them, probably a boozer. The three men left soon after them, then the light was turned on again. A few seconds later, George uttered a long squawk, then nothing until Liz hurried out of the house. She was carrying a large bag. She crossed the street to speak to me; she looked awful. 'I killed that bastard', she said, 'I must go far away from here.' 'Did they rape you?' I asked. 'They did', she said, 'and he tried to hit me with his belt again when they had left home; to punish me!' She had hidden a knife in the bedroom in case he beat and raped her again, so she had knifed him. 'I called the cops', I said. She knew I had, but that didn't matter any more. She wanted to go to the station at once and leave the country. She told me she had friends in France and in Belgium. I saw her off at Waterloo; she had bought a ticket for Paris."

"Did she try to get in touch with you when she was there?"

"I said she could write to me, my tenants give me the mail I receive, well, I don't get much, you know. I got a letter from her last year. She was living in Alsace, and she intended to move to Belgium, somewhere on the eastern coast. She seemed quite happy."

"As far as I understand, George is dead, so he can't possibly have written this letter."

"Who knows? Was he really dead? I believed he was, but..."

"... Was his corpse found?"

"I don't know. I didn't come back to Jubilee Street for a couple of days. I saw, as I was passing by, that nothing seemed to have changed. There was no light at night, no noise. Someone moved in a few months later. I suppose the owner didn't get the money for the rent and he investigated to know what was going on. He had rented the house to another couple who must have left recently."

"What shall I do if George comes back?"

"You live at number 46, so he won't come here. He expects to see her at number 64."

"He should have guessed that she has moved. How can he suppose that she stayed and waited for him in the house after she had knifed him? Why did he leave for Australia? I can't understand. It doesn't make sense."

"I don't get more than you do; what a shaggy dog story it is!"

"Anyway, thank you ever so much for telling me."

"I'm not sure it was the right thing to do. You're even more embarrassed now."

"At least I know what happened."

"That won't lead you very far, and I'm quite worried. If George is alive and comes back here, he might find your address; and who knows what he could do? By the way, do you live alone here?"

"I do."

"Well, you shouldn't stay by yourself."

"He won't come back until two months, if he ever does. I'll have time to think about it."

"Well, I'd better go now. I'll sleep under the porch again... If you feel like talking, or anything else, you'll find me there in the evening, and part of the day."

"All right. Thank you ever so much again. Come and visit me whenever you want."

"O.K. See you."

"See you, Shirley."

During the next two months, they met several times. Elizabeth was busy at work and didn't seem to think much of the letter. Although she sometimes mentioned it, she didn't appear to be concerned. Nevertheless the old woman expected to see George one day. She had been anxious since she had been dreaming of his return to Jubilee Street, by mid-November.

"You can't stay in the streets all winter long!" Elizabeth declared.

"I'm used to it now. It will be the third one in the cold for me," Shirley asserted.

"It's too dangerous. You should come and sleep here when it freezes outside, just like now."

"Don't worry. I'm telling you I'm used to it."

"May I insist? Just a few days, until the temperature rises."

Shirley suddenly thought it wasn't such a bad idea. If he visited Elizabeth, she wouldn't be alone in front of him. She could help better than from outside. It also occurred to her that her young friend was asking her to stay at her place for a while because she was anxious too.

"A few days, you said?"

"You would be fine here!"

"No doubt I will be, but I might enjoy this comfort again and overstay your welcome, dear."

"Do you mean you agree?"

"I will leave as soon as the weather gets better, all right ?"

"All right. Let me take you to your room."

"I haven't slept in a bed for ages! But I'm even more interested in the bathroom, you know. A good old warm shower will do me good!"

Shirley turned out to be a nice companion. She was a rather good cook as well. One morning, someone rang the bell. Elizabeth was at work. Shirley was in the living-room ; she looked through the window and saw a young man she had never seen before. She opened the door and found herself face to face with a smiling guy whom she estimated to be in his late twenties.

"Hello, Madam."

"Hello, Sir."

"Is Elizabeth Jones living here?"

"Who are you, young man?"

"My name is George."

"You can't be George!"

"I beg your pardon, Madam."

"Go away ! Stay away from this house!"

"I... I don't understand. Let me..."

She slammed the door in his face before he had time to finish his sentence. She was reeling from the shock. The man didn't look like George! She sat in the living-room, wondering who else he could be. 'Was he real? Did I have some hallucination?' she asked herself.

She told Elizabeth about the visit as soon as she came back.

"Have you seen anyone in the street? A man who looks like the one who came this morning?"

"I didn't, Shirley. Now, tell me, are you absolutely sure that he isn't George, I mean the one who lived at number 64?"

"Definitely."

"You know, you haven't seen him for over two years. He may have changed his look."

"I'm sure he isn't the George I know."

"What about his voice?"

"His voice?"

"You know his voice, don't you?"

"Of course I do, but I... I didn't pay attention... I was in a state of shock. I'm sorry."

"Never mind. A coincidence, then?"

"How could it be a coincidence? He must be back from Australia by now, and a man called the same name suddenly appears ! It hadn't occurred to me before, but he may have changed his face!"

"What do you mean?"

"Aesthetic surgery ! "Like in 'Dark passage', a film with Humphrey Bogart."

"I haven't seen it."

"Vincent Parry escapes from prison after being unfairly accused of killing his wife." Shirley was suddenly fired with enthusiasm. "He gets a new face from a plastic surgeon to dodge the authorities and find his wife's murderer."

"We're not in a film, Shirley."

"Oh, sorry. I like films with Humphrey Bogart and Lauren Bacall, you know. They played together in that film, and in... Well, don't you think..."

"... I can't believe it. I don't think he had an operation not to be recognized. Otherwise he wouldn't have told you his name!"

"Why not ? He expected to meet Liz and introduce himself as George to frighten her to death. Maybe he wants to make her mad!"

"And he thinks I'm Liz, terrified at the idea that he's back ! If this guy comes again, ask him to come back by six o'clock so that I meet him. When he sees me, he will understand his mistake and leave me alone."

"Don't forget how violent he can be. When he realizes she doesn't live here, he might take his revenge on you. This guy is crazy!"

"Do as I said! It's the only way, and I'm sure you're mistaken."

"All right, but you'll have to be careful."

"Don't worry."

"Nobody came while you were away at work", Shirley said, the next day, "But the phone rang several times."

"Thank you, Shirley. What does the answering machine say?"

She pressed the button and listened.

"Hello Liz, this is your Mum. Don't forget your Dad's birthday on the 25th. Will you spend the whole weekend with us in Reading? Your brother will come from Manchester with his fiancée. They met in Liverpool about six months ago; she's from

Birmingham. We hope you're still fine. Kisses from Mum and Dad. Bye..." "...Hello dear, Anny calling. Will you come around this weekend? Perhaps we could go to the cinema; Daisy told me she might come with us. What about doing some shopping? We haven't been to the shops together for such a long time... Kisses, Anny..." "...Miss Jones? My name is George. I took the opportunity to visit you yesterday morning. Unfortunately you were not in and I was welcome a bit coldly by a lady who wasn't very keen on my name, as far as I understood. I didn't have time to explain the reason for my visit. I actually work as a volunteer for Great Ormond Street Hospital Charity; I'm in charge of visiting our most devoted members. I know you've done a lot for our child patients who appreciate your help a great deal; you've done such a good job so far and we all would like to thank you for both your commitment and donations. So, dear Miss Jones, will you accept to be a guest of honour at our annual party? Be sure we will be highly honoured if you do. Please would you mind calling number 2072393000? I'm George Parris; just leave a message for me if I'm off. Thank you very much indeed. Bye bye."

"Listen to that, Shirley!"

"What is it?"

"A message from George. Come and listen!"

Shirley frowned.

"Come on; listen, please!"

She listened to the message and began to laugh.

"What a fool I have been! How stupid!"

"It's all right, Shirley."

"Will you accept the invitation?"

"I surely will."

"That's fine, Elizabeth. Call Mr Parris and forget how foolish I can be sometimes. An old silly woman!"

"I'm calling him, then we'll have dinner, dear old thing!"

"I think it's about time for the old thing to go back to the street. I need to ventilate my brain, Elizabeth."

"There's no hurry, Shirley."

A few hours later, as they were both asleep, a man who had just arrived in London was standing on the pavement, opposite the street.

Two days later, on a sunny Saturday afternoon, the weather was getting somewhat warmer, so Shirley was thinking of leaving Elizabeth's house. Her host considered that she could stay on for some time.

"Why not one more week?"

"Well, I'm getting used to living here. I told you I won't be able to leave if I stay too long."

"Just wait until the beginning of March."

"Is your hospital party next week?"

"Yes, on Friday night."

"All right, I'll leave on Saturday then. Is that fair enough?

"That's fine."

The man hadn't come back. He knew where Elizabeth was living, which was enough for him to know for the time being.

"She's moved to number 64", he said to three men who were having a drink with him at *the Castle*, a pub in Commercial Road.

"How did you find her?" Roger asked.

"I went to the post office. The guy said he had seen her after she had received my letter. I had actually made a mistake writing the address. By a strange coincidence, I had written '64', where she lives now, instead of '46'. I've been awfully lucky."

"If I were her, I would have moved far away instead of staying in the same street", Roy answered.

"She didn't know if I was dead or alive. She must have left the neighbourhood for some time before coming back. She must have thought that if I recovered from my injury, I would look for her everywhere in the world, except in Jubilee Street."

"A clever girl, isn't she?"

"Sure, but you don't fool George so easily!"

"Well done, George", Gary said. "If you need us for another night party with her, we are your men, aren't we, guys?"

"Do you remember how it ended up the first time? She stabbed me in the stomach and left me for dead. She won't do it again. I'll visit her and I'll kill her!"

"Without having a little chat?" Roy asked.

"You won't get high if you kill her straight away. Have some fun before", Roger said.

"And let us have fun with you. We'll make sure she won't stab anyone, George", Gary added.

"Easy, guys", George said. "You're right. I've been waiting for two years, and I've promised to 'marry' her, haven't I? What a wedding night she will have! And we'll have a whale of a time!"

"Good old George, we thought you had

disappeared, you know, until I got a call from you. When was that, a couple of months after you left for Australia?" Gary said.

"More or less. I didn't call until I had recovered."

"Here you are again, that's the main thing, good old mate. Let's drink to George, fellows. Cheers!"

George hadn't left England on an impulse, but he had been greatly influenced by the man who had found him lying on a pavement in Aylward Street. He had immediately proposed to call number 999, which George had refused. He didn't want to be taken to hospital.

"I see, some old scores have been settled. Let me have a look at the wound."

George knew that doctors and nurses would ask him questions, that the police would visit him again. They knew who he was ; if he told them Liz had knifed him, they would make the connection with a possible rape. She might even lodge a complaint against him and his accomplices. It would be considered that she had acted in self-defence, and they would be sent to jail. Furthermore, he would be seen as responsible for the rape and more severely sentenced than the others.

"It could be worse, mate. Do you know you're a lucky one? I used to be a doc for the Australian army, so I can deal with the matter. Let me take you to my place. It's a bit far, about a quarter of a mile, but you will survive, I'm telling you. My name is Bruce. Come on, mate, let's go."

"I'm George. Thanks a lot, Bruce."

"You're welcome, George."

Bruce dressed the wound, so that his patient was

soon out of danger. A week later, George was feeling better, but he was exhausted.

"You need time to recover; don't worry, in a month, you won't even remember what happened."

"I'll remember Liz."

"She's done a bad thing, but you must forget about it."

George hadn't told Bruce about the whole story indeed. He had missed some major details not to be thought of as the bastard he definitely was. Bruce had to imagine Liz as a kind of vixen the poor guy had had a hard time living with.

"I won't forget."

"What will you do? Kill her and go to prison? I've got a better idea. You told me you were fed up with your boss. You're a bricklayer, aren't you? They need bricklayers in Sydney. I'm going back there in three weeks, do you remember? Come with me!"

Although George was obsessed by Liz, and the revenge he intended to take on her, he was clear-sighted enough to understand that his new friend's proposal deserved to be thought over for it might offer some advantages. He eventually accepted to go to Australia. There he had a good job and had fun in the city bars almost every night. Yet, after one year and a half, his desire to go back to England and kill Liz was so strong that he could hardly think of anything else. He soon made up his mind to leave Australia, and he took great pleasure sending her the letter; if Shirley had been wrong about aesthetic surgery, she had been perfectly right when she had ventured to say that he intended to frighten Liz to death. As for Elizabeth, she wasn't afraid any more.

Whereas Shirley remained on her guard, she was busy thinking of the Friday evening party. She was particularly enthusiastic about being a guest of honour. On Sunday morning, as she liked dressing up, she was in her bedroom, looking for the clothes she could wear for the event, when she heard the bell. She went downstairs to open the door to a man who was holding a bunch of flowers in both hands like a precious object he wouldn't drop for a fortune, as if his own life had depended on it. He was smiling at her. Strictly and neatly dressed though without taste, he was wearing a dark green jacket which was no match for his navy-blue shirt and light green tie, which didn't prevent Elizabeth from liking him at once. She found him funny and was amused at the thought that she should teach him how to get dressed properly.

"Elizabeth! I'm ever so happy to have the opportunity to meet you at last. I have been looking forward to speaking with you again. Well... Let me offer you... Sorry... How rude you must think I am... My name is George..."

"George!"

"Yes, I am George!"

"The same George who came a few days ago and I spoke with on the phone?"

"You are right. I am this George."

"I'm very happy! So I'm Elizabeth, as you already know."

"Of course... George Parris."

"You told me on the phone."

"Did I?"

"You did."

"So I did." He looked and sounded shy; Elizabeth loved that. "Oh, before I forget, otherwise you will think I am such an idiot, will you do me the favour of accepting these flowers?"

"How wonderful, George. Thank you ever so much. Do come in!"

"I didn't mean to disturb you, Elizabeth."

"You don't. Please come in." She was already in the hall, talking to Shirley. "Guess who's visiting us! Look at these flowers; aren't they beautiful? George, have a seat; make yourself comfortable. You've met Shirley, haven't you?"

"We have been... er... introduced, indeed."

"I must apologize to you for being so rude the other day. I mistook you for someone else. You can't imagine how sorry I am!"

"Let's forget it, Shirley."

"What about a cup of tea?" Elizabeth suggested. "I know it isn't tea-time, but I drink a lot of tea!"

"So do I", George answered. "For me, it's tea-time all day long."

"Fine. I think we'll get on well."

"I do hope so."

"Shirley, will you have some tea with us?"

"I'm afraid I can't. I have a lot to do upstairs. Have a good time; I'll see you later."

"She's very nice, you know, in spite of what you may have thought."

"I have no doubt about it."

"It's very nice of you to pay me a visit."

"I am one of your admirers!"

"Do I have so many? I've done nothing to be admired."

"What you have done for all these children for over ten years is absolutely remarkable."

"I'm sure what you do is at least as remarkable as what I've done so far."

"I have been at Great Ormond Street Hospital for only two years. I saw you at the party last year."

"Did you?"

"I even remember the clothes you were wearing. How elegant!"

"Thank you." She could hardly return the compliment, but she felt flattered. He definitely had the most awful taste in the world as for choosing his clothes, but this could be improved providing that a woman should advise him. Yet he had the most wonderful manners, which definitely was far more difficult to learn. He was by no means a good-looking man although he wasn't unpleasant to look at.

"You must have a good memory to remember such details."

"You were so charming, Elizabeth."

She felt some kind of embarrassment, which he seemed to realize, then he changed the subject.

"Let's talk about Friday party, if you don't mind."

"I think it's a good idea."

George, who was taking part in the organization, told Elizabeth how everything had been scheduled; she would be introduced to the audience by the president and be awarded special membership, for which everyone would expect her to make a speech. As she admitted that she was a little frightened, he proposed to accompany her if that was to give her some comfort. She accepted with pleasure.

The two ladies had a quiet time during the week. Elizabeth was getting more and more excited. Her meeting with George Parris had, to a certain extent, boosted her life. She was singing all the time. She woke up in a good mood and went to bed with happy feelings.

The only event to be noticed was Shirley's amazement at seeing a young woman who reminded her of Liz in Jubilee Street. She actually was standing in the front garden when it happened. 'Gosh', she thought, 'I can't believe it'. She hurried back into the kitchen, found the key and locked the door, went through the gate into the street. The woman had paced down in front of number 46, then she had resumed her walk and soon turned right into Stepney Way. Shirley paced up, her heart pounding. It was Friday afternoon and Elizabeth would be back earlier than usual. She had done the housework and prepared a nice meal for the evening. She had already packed her belongings as she was expecting to leave the day after. She found it painful, in a way. In Stepney Way, she could no longer see the woman. She seemed to have vanished.

"Have you seen a young woman in a long red coat, please?" she asked a middle-aged couple.

"A woman in a long red coat? Have you noticed her, Mary?"

"I haven't."

"She was in this street about one minute ago. You can't have missed her!"

"I'm sorry, but my husband and I haven't seen her."

"Never mind. Thank you."

She came back to Jubilee Street, wondering whether she was getting mad. 'You must have been dreaming, my poor Shirley', she said to herself. She decided not to tell Elizabeth. They had dinner together, feeling both happy and a little sad.

"I will feel lonely without you."

"You've been used to living alone for a long time now; for longer than I."

"I know, but I'll feel strange for at least a few days, you know. Maybe human beings aren't supposed to live on their own."

"It's possible, but you may not stay alone forever. You might even find yourself in good company sooner than you think."

"What do you mean?"

"I mean you're attracted by Mr Parris."

"I like him. He's been very nice to me."

"You don't only like him, and he is in love with you."

"He hardly knows me!"

"He knows you enough to love you, anyway. And don't tell me you aren't fond of him!"

"I admit I am."

"So you don't need me, and it's all very well like that."

"Whatever may happen, don't forget you will always be welcome here."

"I know that, and I promise I'll visit you."

"I hope so."

"Well, you'd better get ready before George arrives. Have a nice evening."

"Thank you, Shirley. Have a nice evening too."

In the meantime, the four men were at George's place, each with a glass of white wine to go with fish and chips. A young woman was having steak and kidney pie at the 'Anchor'. As for George Parris, he had put on his best suit, actually a dark blue one, a purple shirt and a yellow tie with cats and dogs on it, and was about to take his brand new crepe rubber thick-soled shoes out of a cupboard.

Jubilee Street was in each of these people's mind as a common destination, with different purposes. Mr Parris was there long before the others. By half past seven, he parked his car in front of number 64. There was a little fog; the canopy of heaven seemed lower than usual. It wasn't really cold, but the air was damp. He had put his overcoat on. It was only a few minutes later when Elizabeth and he left for Guilford Street. It took them about half an hour to get there. The hospital car park was almost full when they arrived. A lot of people were already gathering together in the main hall.

Elizabeth met some of her acquaintances, then George introduced her to a few friends of his, especially Lucia, a lady of Spanish origin he worked with.

"I'm so glad to meet you, Elizabeth. I've heard so much about you."

"I'm afraid there isn't so much to say about me."

"George told me a lot! You're doing such a great deal for our Charity!"

"I'm doing my best, but it's the least one can do for these children."

At that moment, the chairman, who was standing on the stage, started speaking.

"Ladies and gentlemen, dear friends, I am so happy to welcome you tonight."

The whole assembly was listening silently. He made a long speech, then he introduced the three guests of honour in turns. Elizabeth came in second position.

"Now, I am proud to welcome a lady whose devotion has long been known by many of us; a lady whose involvement in our Children's Charity has always been sincere and selfless... Miss Elizabeth Jones!"

He led a long round of applause for her.

"Elizabeth, thanks to people like you, I allow myself to say, today, that Great Ormond Street Hospital Charity, which has been so successful so far, is also promised to the most glorious future."

She was moved to tears.

"Dear Elizabeth, will you please do us the favour of becoming a life honorary member of our Charity?"

She hardly could believe her ears.

"Sir, I can't tell... you how flattered... I mean... how honoured I am. Indeed I happily agree to become a life member.... And I thank you ever so much for that. I will go on doing my best to help you, as long as I can, and I do hope we will carry out the greatest achievements together."

"Thank you ever so much, Elizabeth."

There was another great applause. "What a day", she said to herself, "I will always remember this night."

George Parris wasn't the least happy man in the audience. As for the other George, he was coming out of his flat with his friends. The four of them were half drunk. Roy, a bottle of vodka in his hand, was singing.

"Shut up", Gary said.

"Come on, Gary!"

"That's enough", Roger said, "Get into the car."

They had a long way to drive to Jubilee Street, though the traffic was light. It had started to rain; it didn't stop until they reached their destination. Roy had fallen asleep; he woke up when the car stopped.

Shirley was coming out of the bathroom. It was ten o'clock. The men were walking on the pavement; they were silent.

"She's in", George said, "She's not in bed yet. We'll have to wait."

"Go back to the car", Roger suggested, "I'll hide in the garden, and I'll let you know when we can go in."

"That's OK. Roy, Gary, come on."

'One more comfortable night', Shirley said to herself, 'I might regret it... Well, I made my mind to live on the streets two years ago, I mustn't forget it." She went to bed and turned out the light. Outside, Roger waited a couple of minutes, then he went to tell the others.

"All right, guys. The road is clear. Gary, pass me the crowbar."

"Roy has got it."

"Pass it to me."

"Don't worry, I can handle it; I will open that bloody door."

"Pass it to Roger!", George ordered to him.

"Do you think I am..."

"I think you're drunk. Roger will open the door, all right?"

Roy got out of the Vauxhall and reluctantly handed the crowbar to Roger.

It didn't take long to force the door open. They entered and checked the ground floor.

"Let's go upstairs", George whispered.

A step creaked under his weight. He stopped and waited, motionless. Then he went up again, making slow progress. When he had reached the first floor, he turned his lamp towards the others for them to climb the stairs in turns. He proceeded to the first room and found it empty; he opened the next door and heard a snore.

"Here we are, at last !" he murmured, "Ready, guys? Put on the light and let's have fun!"

One of them searched for the switch. Before he could find it, George began to speak aloud.

"How are you, my dear Elizabeth? It's been such a long time. Here we are again! You and me, and our friends, of course!"

"Who are you?" Shirley screamed, just as Gary was turning the light on.

"Who's that old hag?" Roy shouted.

"Shut up!" George replied, "Where's Liz?"

"I know who you are", Shirley said, "I've known you for a long time, and you, cowards!" She got up while speaking to them; she didn't look or sound frightened. "You raped her one night, do you remember?"

"What are you talking about?" Roger asked. "That's all nonsense!"

"It does make sense, but the woman you raped

doesn't live here. She left, just after that terrible night, and never came back. George..."

"How do you know my name?"

"It doesn't matter. You've knocked at the wrong door, anyway. My name actually is Elizabeth Jones, but I'm not the one you expected to meet. Liz and I aren't related; we just happened to know each other, by chance. You'd better go away now, guys!"

"She's lying", Roy shouted again.

"Shut up, Roy." George said; then, turning to Shirley, "Where's Liz? You know where she is, don't you?"

"I've told you; she left and never came back. Nobody in the neighbourhood knows where she is. Leave me alone; piss off!"

"She knows we've raped the other bitch. She'll give us away to the police!" Roy had picked up the crowbar downstairs and was now threatening Shirley.

"Take that crazy bastard away!" she cried.

"Roy, don't!" George said, "She could have told the police long ago if... Don't..." It was too late. The crowbar had smashed Shirley's head.

"What have you done?" Roger rushed at Roy and began to punch his face.

"Stop it", Gary said. "Stop it! We must go now. Let's hurry!"

"Gary's right", George said, "Let's go. Don't forget the crowbar!"

They abandoned Shirley who was lying on the floor, a pool of blood around her head, and left Jubilee Street in a flash. The young woman, who had taken the underground from the 'Anchor', saw them run out of the house.

"I'll be home soon", Elizabeth said to George, "Thank you for taking me to the party, and..."

"Don't mention it, my dear Elizabeth. Did you spend a nice evening?"

"I couldn't have expected a nicest evening; it was absolutely wonderful. I'll tell Shirley about it tomorrow morning; I don't want to wake her at that time."

"She may not be asleep. It is midnight, and I suppose that on the streets, she is used to getting asleep much later."

"You know, on the streets she sleeps any time of the day or night. At home, it's different; she has a more regular life."

"Here we are, Elizabeth!"

He helped her out of his estate car, and they entered the garden.

"Well, George", she said, "I don't know what to say... You've been so nice, and this party was so wonderful."

"It has been a pleasure for me... Have a good night, Elizabeth."

"Thank you, George."

"I will call you tomorrow, if you allow me."

"Of course, I'll be delighted", she answered while taking her keys out of her pocket. "Oh... George..."

"Elizabeth?"

"It's strange!"

"What's the matter?"

"The door is open!"

She switched on the light.

"Someone has broken it. Look!" she exclaimed,

"Good heavens! Shirley!"

"Is she upstairs?" George asked.

"She should be. I'll see if she's in her room. Shirley! Can you hear me? Shirley!"

George followed Elizabeth upstairs.

"This is her room."

George opened the door and stepped in.

"Oh, God", he shouted. He knelt near the lifeless woman to check her pulse, then he turned towards Elizabeth and declared sadly, "I'm really sorry!"

Elizabeth couldn't utter a word. She came next to Shirley and touched her face softly.

"We have to call the police", George said gently after a while.

Elizabeth stood up like a robot and went down to the living-room. She picked up the phone and called the police station. Two inspectors arrived less than fifteen minutes later. She told them the whole story about Shirley and Liz, the letter she had received and what she knew about the foul murder that had just taken place.

"Poor Shirley", she said, "She had decided to leave this morning to go back and live on the streets."

She couldn't help sobbing.

"I persuaded her to stay one more week! I shouldn't have done that; she would still be alive."

"You couldn't expect such a dreadful crime", George answered, "You did your best to help her, as you do with everyone!"

"You have nothing to reproach yourself for, miss", inspector Whismore said, "On top of that, they could have killed you as well if you had been here. The party you attended last night has probably saved your life!"

"You know, sir inspector, it can also be thought that my presence would have saved Shirley's life, and I would be alive, too."

"Let me allow myself to be doubtful of the fact that they would not have killed you, my dear", George answered.

"They would have realized that I'm not Liz, and they would probably have left us alone!"

"Don't forget they haven't hesitated to kill your friend!" inspector Whismore declared, "Anyway, according to the footprints on the stairs, they were at least two. They may actually have been four. The thing is, you know, we'll have some difficulty identifying them."

Elizabeth was now walking to and fro in the living-room, wondering what had really happened. She was convinced that the four men had been present the evening before, just like the night when they had raped Liz. The forensic expert stated that she had died instantly, as a result of a hard knock on the head. The murder weapon hadn't been found.

"We may establish", inspector Barnes, Whismore's colleague, suggested, "that a crowbar has been used to force the entrance door open. It is the kind of tool burglars generally use. We may also think that it has been used to kill the victim."

"It is so horrible!" Elizabeth said, still crying.

"Miss Jones", inspector Whismore said, "The ambulance men are taking the corpse to the Royal London Hospital. As for us, we're going to leave you now. I think you'd better not stay alone for the rest of the night, and maybe the days to come."

"Thank you very much, but I don't think these men will ever come back. I can stay on my own."

"It's up to you", the inspector answered.

Everybody soon left, except George, who insisted that she shouldn't remain without protection.

"It's four in the morning. You should go home now. You must be awfully tired."

"Certainly not more than you are. Go to bed, I'll stay here to stand guard. I'll call a locksmith as soon as morning comes."

Before leaving, some policemen had blocked up the front door which still had to be repaired.

"You can't sleep in this armchair."

"Why not?"

"You won't be comfortable."

"Don't worry, go and get some sleep now."

"I'm so happy you are here, George."

"I am so happy to help you."

She came closer to him and laid her head upon his shoulder. He didn't really know what to do; he was feeling rather embarrassed.

"See you later," she said with a smile, as she was slowly moving away from him.

"Good night, Elizabeth."

"Good night, George."

Elizabeth woke up with a start in the morning. Someone was making noise downstairs. When she heard George's voice, she understood that he was speaking with the locksmith who was fixing the door. It had taken her a long time to fall asleep. She had been thinking of Shirley, of her violent death. She couldn't help thinking that it could have been different; yet she had to accept the fact that she was dead. She had been a real friend although they hadn't known each other for a long time.

She got up and went to the bathroom. She felt weary. She was looking forward to having a bath, as if she had herself been stained by those criminals; as if she had been raped instead of Liz, as if she had been slain instead of Shirley. She had become an actor in the play when she had opened that bloody letter! The night before had reached a climax of horror; it had started like a dream to end in a nightmare.

She was feeling a little better when she came downstairs for breakfast.

"Oh, George, you must have had a terrible night! It seems that you woke up early."

"I did. The locksmith has already finished his job. I called him at dawn and I explained to him under which circumstances this had been done. He didn't hesitate to come straight away."

"It's very nice of him. Did he leave an invoice for me?"

"Don't worry about that. He happens to be a fellow whom I have been acquainted with for long. He didn't wish to bother you, so he will send the invoice to you in a few days."

"Wonderful! What would I do without your help? Please come and have breakfast!"

"Well, I must admit I am not really hungry."

"Neither am I. We must have something yet; a cup of tea or coffee and some toast will do us good."

"You are perfectly right. You are a courageous woman."

"I'm not courageous."

"You definitely are."

"I am just facing up to the situation because I have to. I would betray the memory of Shirley if I didn't. I must organize her funeral."

"I will do my best to help you take all the necessary steps."

"You have already done a tremendous lot for me. I think you should go home to have a bath and a rest."

"All right, but I will come back in the afternoon, otherwise I will be awfully worried. It is not safe for you to stay on your own."

"I promise I will be careful. It's OK for this afternoon."

"Will three o'clock be alright?"

"That'll be perfect."

"So I'll see you this afternoon, Elizabeth. Lock the door behind me."

"I will. Bye, George."

"Goodbye, Elizabeth."

As soon as he had left, she called her parents and told them what had happened. Her mother immediately proposed to come to London.

"You know it's no trouble at all for us. We'll pack our luggage this morning and we'll be in London in the middle of the afternoon. We'll stay as long as necessary. We won't feel easy until the police have caught those criminals."

"Thank you very much. I will feel better with you at home. Although I'm sure that they won't come back, I'll be afraid when night comes."

"That's perfectly understandable, my dear. Good

luck for all you have to do this morning. We'll be in London as soon as possible. Bye bye, dear."

"Bye, mum. See you this afternoon."

She was about to leave for the hospital when someone rang the doorbell. Through the spyhole she recognized inspector Whismore and let him in.

"Good morning, miss Jones. I wanted to make sure you had spent a quiet night."

"They didn't come back, if it's what you were worried about."

"This is not surprising. Oh, I see the door has been fixed, that's a good thing."

"Will you have something to drink? Tea? Coffee?"

"No, thank you. I don't mean to bother you."

"You don't. By the way, Shirley gave me the address of a notary, just in case something nasty happened to her. Shall I call him or will you do that?"

"I can do it for you. She owned a house in Jamaica Street, didn't she ?"

"She did."

"You told me she had no relative, no friend you might get in touch with."

"Nobody except Liz."

"Maybe the notary will be able to give me someone's name. I will let you know if he does. I'm going to pay him a visit this morning, but I will go and see her tenants first. Oh, do you know if she had a bank account?"

"I think so, although we never really discussed the matter. All I am certain is that her tenants gave her some cash every month."

"Did she carry that money with her?"

"She actually did."

"I'll ask my colleagues if they have found it in her personal belongings when I get back to the police station. I might come back this afternoon, if you don't mind."

"I'll be back from the Royal Hospital. My parents are coming to spend some time with me, and George will come around."

"Good. I'll see you this afternoon then. Goodbye, miss Jones."

"Goodbye, sir inspector."

Elizabeth had a hard time at the hospital. When she suddenly faced the reality of a death certificate a nurse was handing to her, she realized that she would never see Shirley alive again. She had seen some children pass away before. She had accompanied a few until the second when they had died. Yet she had never been through the following step, between the death and the funeral.

She spent little time with the undertaker who drew up an estimate and called the notary for his agreement about the expense for the funeral. As things had been settled, she walked back home.

Her parents arrived by half past two, then George visited her, preceding Inspector Whismore.

"I don't mean to bother you indeed, Miss Jones. As a matter of fact, I just want to let you know that everything is all right with the notary. Apart from that, some money has been found in Mrs Nelson's bag, which may confirm that the men who came last night had no intention to rob."

"They meant to kill Elizabeth!" Mrs Jones said.

"Not precisely. They may have intended to kill

another Elizabeth Jones."

"What difference does it make?"

"Please, mum!"

"We are investigating, Madam. I hope we'll find some clue very soon. Well, I must leave now. Have a nice weekend!"

Inspector Whismore left. Everyone in the house was worried.

On Sunday morning, Mr Jones had a walk in the area. On the way, he passed in front of a newsagent's and read 'the Whitechapel murder" on the front page of a popular newspaper. He stopped to buy it, and resumed his way to Jubilee Street. Back home, he started reading the article.

The police seem to have obtained no clue to the perpetrator of the murder which took place last night in a house situated in Jubilee Street. There is at the moment, it must be acknowledged, no ground for blaming the officers in charge should they fail in unravelling the mystery surrounding the crime.

The murder, in the late hours of Friday evening, of a woman known as Shirley Nelson, is believed to be the work of several men. Yet only one seems to have hit her, once, with a crowbar, robbery being no motive for the crime since her fellow-lodger, the owner of the house, declared that nothing had been stolen. She was the last person who saw her alive by half past seven, when she left for an evening party. She found the body when she returned home and is positive as to the time being eleven. Detective inspectors Whismore and Barnes are in charge of the case on behalf of the Criminal Investigation Department.

He called Elizabeth and her mother who were busy upstairs.

"What's going on, Peter?"

"It's about a newspaper article."

"A newspaper article?" Elizabeth asked, "Does it deal with Shirley's murder?"

"It does, actually."

They both came downstairs and went through the journalist's report.

"The Whitechapel murder!" Mr Jones pointed out, "It's as if Jack the Ripper were back, except that he killed younger women he chose in the street."

"Peter ! You're frightening Elizabeth!"

Somewhere in Darnley Street, in Hackney, Gary was visiting Roger. He had also bought the morning newspaper.

"Read this, Roger!"

"It's about the murder, isn't it?"

"Sure."

"God, someone else is living in the house! A woman!"

"And she must be Liz!"

"She is! The old bitch was a bloody liar! We must show it to George!"

"He may have read it already."

"Never mind. Let's go!"

They walked to Kenton Road, a few streets away. George had actually read the article.

"She lied!" Gary exclaimed.

"I know she did."

"What are we doing now, George?"

"Nothing."

"What about your fucking Liz?"

"Come on, Gary; George is right. There's nothing we can do for the time being."

"Nobody has seen us! The old cow is dead!"

"Fortunately", George answered, "I was furious when Roy killed her, but he's helped us in a way. Let's wait for things to calm down, then we will see."

"OK, George", Gary answered grudgingly.

"What about Roy? Have you seen him?" Roger asked.

"I saw him this morning. He is keeping a low profile."

"Let's hope he will say nothing which might let people think that..."

"... Don't worry. He's quiet now. I'm sure he'll be all right, just like us. We just have to go on living as before; and if someone, at work for instance, drops a hint about what happened the other night, we just don't answer. Not a single word!"

The police kept investigating, but found no clue. Shirley's burial took place on Tuesday afternoon. Few people attended the ceremony. Some members of Great Ormond Hospital Charity had come to comfort Elizabeth. George Parris was one of them indeed. He had made the habit of visiting her every day, which undoubtedly pleased her a lot. Although she was really sad, her daily life wasn't unpleasant. She had good relations with her parents, she was doing well at her job, and her happiest moments were those she spent with him.

On Saturday morning, the newspapers reported

another murder, in Hackney this time. The victim was a man called Gary Smith. He had died in his own flat, poisoned. The police might have thought of a suicide had they not found the word 'rapist' tagged on his tee-shirt, which brought evidence that someone had helped him die.

"What an unfortunate period", Mr Jones commented.

"Don't you think it has always been the same, and this has nothing to do with our period?" his daughter suggested.

"Things are getting worse, my dear."

"According to your father, the world gets darker every day, people are becoming crazy, and half the population is about to kill the other half!" Mrs Jones said.

"You see, Janet", he answered, "The problem with you is that you hardly understand the world you live in."

"I may not understand..."

"... Stop!" Elizabeth intervened, "Stop quarrelling, please! I don't want to hear about crimes any more!"

"You prefer hearing about Mr Parris, don't you, my dear?" Mrs Jones remarked.

Elizabeth blushed a little.

"Let's prepare something for lunch!" she proposed.

"A most refined gentleman, extremely good-hearted. The perfect husband for a distinguished young lady, but..."

"...Mum!"

"Oh, don't tell me you haven't noticed how ill-inspired he is for choosing his clothes!"

"I've noticed it, mum."

"You know, when your father and I met, it was about the same. He had no taste at all, but I educated him."

"You must be joking, Janet."

"I'm not. Since we were married, you've been much more elegantly dressed, haven't you?"

"You didn't educate me for all that, my dear. You've just been choosing my clothes, and I must say I've never had to complain about this."

Elizabeth was laughing.

"It's time for cooking, mum, and stop talking as if George and I were about to get married."

"Don't worry, she won't!" Her father answered.

'A funny couple they are', Elizabeth thought, 'but they get on so well, in fact. How lucky I am!"

Contrary to her, George, Roy and Roger had read the article with a great deal of attention. They were particularly worried about the way Gary's murder had been set up.

"The police will probably find our names in his address book!"

"They will question us", Roy said, "We may be accused of killing Gary!"

"George and I have killed nobody so far!" Roger quietly answered, "We all have alibis anyway. Most worrying is 'rapist', which was written by the murderer. It proves that he or she knows us. Not only him, but the four of us!"

"What strikes me", George went on, "is that he has been poisoned. So he let the person in without being suspicious. I know what's in your mind,

Roger, but he would have recognized Liz!"

"He wouldn't have let her in! I quite agree about that, but I say the murderer knows that we raped Liz!"

"Someone may have seen us!" Roy suggested.

"We came out of the house in a hurry, all right. We didn't look around us, but it was dark and this 'someone' can't possibly have seen our faces", Roger answered.

"Maybe there was someone else in the house. We didn't check the other room upstairs."

"Come on, Roy. The owner was out that night and came back by eleven. There was no one else in the house. What do you think, George?"

"I don't know what to think any more. All I know is that we must be very careful from now on. Gary came first on the list. One of us must be second, or one of you two!"

"Why not you?" Roy asked.

"Because I'm sure the murderer knows about my relationship with Liz and will keep me as number four!"

In the afternoon, Elizabeth and George were having a walk in Victoria Park, north of Bethnal Green area.

"I have been looking forward to spending a whole afternoon with you," he declared.

"We're spending plenty of time together", she answered.

"Yes, but this time we are alone. I like your parents very much, of course, and I am always extremely happy to have a talk with them..."

"... I understand. I enjoy being alone with you,

too. It's as if I were coming back to normal life, thanks to you."

"You're being so nice to me. I hope this is... How can I say? It is, you know, a little embarrassing..."

She looked at him, motionless.

"... I mean, Elizabeth, that I hope this is just a beginning."

"Of what?"

She was smiling at him in such a charming way.

"Of a long relationship!"

"I do hope so, too."

"I know, Elizabeth, that we have known each other for quite a short time, but..."

"... But?"

George was feeling shy.

"It is really difficult to say, you know."

"Don't, if it's too hard to say for the moment."

"You may be right."

"Anyway, what change will it make? You'd better tell me right now!"

"I hope you will not regret it."

"You won't regret it, George."

They were so close to each other that he had no difficulty to attract her towards him and kiss her.

"Hum! Things are quite clear like this."

"I apologize for the offhand manner..."

"I like your offhand manner! Would you mind trying again?"

He kissed her again. Their embrace lasted longer this time.

Although Elizabeth considered there was no reason why her parents should stay any longer, they decided it was too soon for them to leave her. They enjoyed visiting London sites every afternoon. Although they knew nothing about her love affair with George, Mr and Mrs Jones couldn't but realize that she was in the best mood, and had no doubt about the origin of this sudden change.

The two lovers had plans for the following weekend. They were about to leave for Cambridge on Saturday morning when inspector Whismore came to inform them that a man had been shot dead in Hackney the night before.

"It is the second one in a week, and a relation might exist between these crimes and Mrs Nelson's death."

"What do you mean, sir inspector?" George asked, impatient to know.

"First, although the first murder wasn't committed in the same area, one must notice that they all took place on Friday nights."

"Do you think those who killed Shirley have also murdered the two other people?" Elizabeth inquired.

"Not exactly. I mean that the two men who were killed in Hackney may have murdered your friend, miss Jones. Last week, my colleagues found the word 'rapist' tagged on Mr Gary Smith's tee-shirt. As a matter of fact, last night they found the word 'murderer' on Mr Roger Hunt's shirt. So the murderer is trying to avenge someone, maybe Liz and Shirley! Furthermore, each time he or she called the police for them to find the corpse."

"It does make sense", George said, "But who do you think that mysterious avenger might be?"

"I don't know, but inspector Hartford, from

Hackney, let me know that those two had two close friends whom they often went to a local pub with; Roy Matthew and George Parkins."

"George Parkins!" Elizabeth repeated.

"Have you ever heard this name before, miss Jones?"

"Never. It's just... George!"

"Of course, four men, one of them known as George, but Mrs Nelson never told you about the surname of the man who used to live with Liz!"

"She probably didn't know it!"

"That's unfortunate. Those two guys had perfect alibis for the first murder. Inspector Barnes is at Hackney police station at the moment and he will call me here, if you don't mind, to tell me how things are going on there."

Inspector Barnes actually called to give inspector Whismore some information a bit later.

"As I suspected, Mr Parkins has a perfect alibi once again. When questioned about Jubilee street, he answered he had never come around. As for Mr Matthew, he wasn't at home this morning. He might be spending his weekend away from London!"

"There must be something you can do", Elizabeth insisted.

"Yes, find evidence against Mr Parkins", he answered.

"Did you try the owner of the house he is supposed to have lived in, in this street?"

"Of course we did. He had only one name to give us; Elizabeth Jones! He didn't even know about the existence of a man living with her."

"So you've got absolutely nothing to prove his

guilt!"

"Nothing, I'm afraid."

Elizabeth and George decided not to put off their day at Cambridge. They had wished it would be romantic, and it actually happened to be.

George Parkins had just come back home after a whole Monday at work, when the phone rang.

"Hello! Who's speaking? Roy! Where have you been all this time? I tried to call you a hundred times this weekend!"

"I know who the murderer is."

"What? Who is it?"

"I can't tell you more on the phone; I think I know where he is now. Come as quickly as you can."

"Why don't you come here?"

"Because I'm hurt; I had a fight with him. You can come faster."

"All right, I'm coming."

"OK. George."

"Before leaving, George took his gun. It could be a trap in which he was bound to fall. He drove to Roy's place. He looked around after getting off his car, as if the street had been involved in the whole story. He entered the building and went up to the third floor. 'Come in. The door is open', he heard after knocking at the door. He stepped into the living-room and stopped short. Roy was tied to a chair, his head down, a knife stabbed in his chest. As he was reading 'rapist' and 'murderer' on his friend's sweater and was taking his gun out, he received a hard blow on the neck and fell unconscious.

When he woke up, he was lying on a bed, feeling

dizzy.

"Liz?"

"Yes, dear."

He tried to get up, but he felt paralyzed.

"What have you done to me?"

"I injected some curarising drug to you. I sort of anaesthetized you, but don't worry, you'll remain conscious, which will give me the opportunity to tell you how I found you and your horrible mates, how I killed them and the way I will kill you!"

"You're a monster!"

"Please don't reverse our roles! By the way, the voice you heard when you knocked actually was Roy's, but it came from a tape-recorder. That poor Roy died after your phone conversation. Very unfortunate, isn't it? Let me tell you the whole story now. Do you mind if I sit comfortably?"

She sat in an armchair. He tried to move again.

"Don't, George, it's absolutely useless. You can't do anything against me, as I couldn't do anything against four men who were raping me, do you remember? I'm sure you do. I'm even wondering if you don't regret a little now. Well, listen to me!"

"Kill me! Kill me now!"

"My poor George! You really have no imagination at all. Let me savour this moment, please. I came back to London a few weeks ago. I thought you were dead, although I wasn't totally sure I had killed you. I went to Jubilee Street the day after my arrival; I was looking for Shirley."

"Shirley?"

"Yes. The one you killed! You know, when things were going so badly between you and me, there was an old woman beggar who was sleeping under the porch, opposite our house. She witnessed most of our arguments and came to see me one day. We had been fighting the night before. She knew you had hit me and was worried about my condition. We became friends. She knew when you four raped me, when I stabbed you before going away to France, then to Belgium. What about you, George? Did you stay in London? How did you survive?"

"Fuck off!"

"It's up to you to shorten the conversation. The less you will participate, the faster you will die!"

"You fucking bitch!"

"Was I a fucking bitch when I was on all fours and you shouted 'come on, Roger, give her a bloody fuck'?"

She stood up and gave him a hard slap in the face. His upper lip started bleeding.

"Go on, Liz. Do it now!"

"Don't tempt me, George!"

"Will you manage this time?"

"I know what you're trying to do', she said quietly, "You're expecting me to lose my temper, but it won't work. Let's come back to our story, if you don't mind. That day, I didn't see Shirley; she wasn't in the place where she used to be. So I decided to go back to Jubilee Street on a Friday night, and guess who I saw there!"

George kept silent.

"You understand, don't you? I saw four old balls running out of a house. It was dark, all right, but it immediately reminded me of that bloody night! I wanted to know what you had done, so I went to

Shirley's porch and I waited. A bit later, I saw a car that stopped in front of the house, then two people entered. Twenty minutes later, the police was there. So I left the street and bought the paper on the morrow. I found the article about Shirley's assassination, and I promised to myself that you wouldn't harm anybody from then on."

"Shirley's death was an accident! Roy, that bastard, killed her! I tried to prevent him, but..."

"... Dear George, how good you are! did you break into the house by accident as well?"

"I swear I didn't mean to do her any harm!"

"What do you expect? That I will forgive you? Are you afraid of dying? Sudden fear, Georgie?"

"Don't call me Georgie. You know I hate that."

"All right. After all, a man's last wishes have to be respected!"

"Go to hell!"

"You'll go there before me... Elizabeth Jones! The young woman who's living there, who made friends with Shirley too, is my homonym! So you expected to find me there! What did you intend to do to me?"

He tried to turn his head towards the wall.

"Look at me, George! Look at me!" She bent over him and grabbed his chin. "How does it feel to be defenceless?"

She sat on the chair again and went on.

"You probably meant to rape me once more, just for fun, then in the middle of the night you would have slain me. A poor woman would have been found in the nude, a prostitute maybe, awfully mutilated by George the Ripper!"

"I wish I had killed you long ago."

"You didn't! When I went to the pub you used to go to, the Dove Free House in Hackney, you didn't recognize me, did you? How amazed you look!"

"That's enough. I don't give a damn fuck about all that story!"

"You must listen to me. You can't leave the stage in the middle of the play, can you? And you don't need to be so rude, you know!"

Liz said to herself that she was such a bitch with him! She was behaving so dreadfully! Nevertheless he deserved it, and she wouldn't step back. She had killed the three others; she had to finish the job anyway.

"I had put a wig on and I was wearing glasses. I looked quite different with short hair, a blue dress, grey stockings, flat-heeled shoes and a red coat on."

"It's impossible. I would have recognized you."

"But you didn't!"

"How did you manage to kill my mates?"

"I see you're interested in the matter at last! It was easier than you think. I followed each of them to know where they were living. After that, it wasn't difficult to charm them one by one. With Gary, I pretended I had fainted. I was lying on the pavement when he arrived in front of his flat. He helped me, of course, and I recovered little by little. He found me so cute that he invited me for a drink in his flat."

"There must have been some witnesses."

"It was nightfall, you know, and it was rather cold. There was nobody in the street."

"And you bloody poisoned him!"

"When he asked me what I wanted to drink, I just

answered 'the same as you'. 'Whisky', he said. 'OK for a whisky', I said. I was doing my best to be as charming as possible."

"I suppose that you dropped the poison in his glass!"

"I suppose so !"

"You suppose so! What a bloody joke!"

"I claimed I had lost my keys on the pavement. I stood up and pretended I was about to faint again. So he proposed to fetch the keys. A perfect example of gallantry. The kind of man who by no means would rape a poor weak woman! And while he was downstairs..."

"I'll kill you, beast!"

"You may intend to, but I must remind you that you can't! Poor old Gary died a few minutes later. It was quite violent, but he didn't suffer very long! As for Roger..."

"Shut up!"

"It's up to you, but if I shut up, I'll have to make you shut up for eternity at once."

She opened her bag and took out a gun.

"The one I used for Roger. I put a pillow on his face – he actually was in his bed – and I shot him. It muffled the noise. For you, there will be no pillow because I want you to look me in the eye when I shoot you. So I've brought a silencer especially for you, my dear George."

"Go to hell, you fucking old cow!"

"Are you ready?"

He suddenly looked at her with an expression of fear. For a second, she felt sorry for him."

In the meantime, Elizabeth was on the phone

with George Parris.

"I'll be delighted to see you tomorrow for lunch. Shall we go to Regent's Park?" she suggested.

"Great", he answered. "It's a wonderful idea."

"Inspector Whismore called me this afternoon. As the police expect another murder on Friday night, they will shadow Mr Parkins and Mr Hunt all day long, and all night long if necessary."

"Have they found Mr Matthew?"

"Not yet."

"You know, if I were the murderer, or the person who has taken the law into her own hands, as far as I may suggest, I would be careful. I wouldn't act on Friday night."

"I said it to the inspector. He answered that the police couldn't watch them all the time; they have other serious cases to deal with. The main thing is that they found some evidence against the two men."

"You are perfectly right, but I'm afraid the investigation is getting bogged down."

"Well, I really hope it will progress."

"And what about your parents? Are they still visiting London?"

"Yes, but they are always with me when I'm at home. They look after me."

"I think they are doing a very good job. I like them."

"I must say they like you too. They appreciate your company ever so much!"

"I'm really happy to know that. Don't forget to say hello for me."

"I won't, George. I'll see you tomorrow then."

"Oh, another thing that you mustn't forget, my dear Elizabeth..."

"What is it?"

"I love you."

"I love you too."

"Have a nice time with your parents this evening. Goodbye, Elizabeth."

"Thank you, have a nice evening. Goodbye."

Whereas Elizabeth was surfing on the wave of happiness, Liz's face was clouded with sadness. She hated George for what he had done. She had loved him and he had wasted her feelings away.

"Liz, I didn't want..."

"... No, George!"

She turned round so that he couldn't see her any more. She wouldn't show her emotion, she wouldn't give him the slightest hope of making her feel pity for him.

"Liz, please..."

"Shut up, George!"

She turned her head in his direction and quickly stretched out her hand, then she pulled the trigger.

As usual, she called the police afterwards, putting on a gruff voice, to warn them. She soon left the flat and disappeared in the darkness of the night.

Later that evening, Elizabeth was asleep when the telephone rang. She first wondered who was bothering her close to midnight, then she thought somebody obviously had important news for her and hurried downstairs.

"Hello, who's speaking?"

"Inspector Whismore. I'm sorry if I woke you up,

but I have to tell you that Matthew and Parkins have been found dead."

"Both dead?"

"Yes, they were both at Matthew's place. He was stabbed through the heart and Parkins was shot."

"So the four have been killed, haven't they?"

"I think there is no danger for you now. The murderer most probably wanted to put a fast end to this story. In a way, if those men were Mrs Nelson's killers, and I dare say I am almost certain about it, he or she somehow protected you."

"I'm glad to know that, but I'm so fed up with all those crimes, you know..."

"... I understand. I think that you will be able to think of more pleasant things from now on. I wish you good night, Miss Jones."

"Thank you for calling. Goodbye, sir inspector."

Elizabeth gave a short account of the event to her parents who had come out of their room in wonder. They were relieved at the news.

"Will you call George?" her mother asked.

"I'd better not. I'll call him in the morning, before leaving for work."

"That sounds quite sensible", her father added, and they all went back to bed.

London, February 18th

Dear Elizabeth,

We have never met, but we had a friend in common, as well as our names.
I think you have understood that George Parkins and his friends intended to kill me when they broke into a house which they thought I was living in. You were lucky enough to be out, but Shirley was unfortunately murdered. You must also know that these four men, whom I saw running out of your house as I happened to be in Jubilee Street, hoping to see Shirley somewhere, raped me over two years ago.
Justice had to be done. I knew the police wouldn't arrest them, and you were likely to be their next victim. So I did it myself.
I visited Shirley's grave yesterday and I left some flowers there. Would you be so kind as to water them for a few days, please, for I must go back from where I came from.

Farewell,

Liz Jones

When Elizabeth folded the letter and put it back into the envelope, she knew that she would keep the secret forever as well as Liz had known she would when she had written to her. She disagreed with her behaviour, but she understood and had a lot of respect for her. Although Liz was a murderess, she wouldn't judge a woman who had clearly suffered a lot.

Her parents were about to leave London; they had loaded their luggage in the car. She went upstairs to hide the letter in her bedroom, then she thanked them for what they had done and they said goodbye.

"Just one thing", Mrs Jones said as her husband had already started the engine, "When we see you and George again, promise me he will be better dressed!"

This remark she had expected brought a smile to Elizabeth's face.

"I promise, mum. I'll have plenty of time to teach him good taste!"

THE PAINTER

William was a painter. He was walking to and fro in his studio in search of inspiration. The more he searched for it, the less he found it. He had neither drawn nor painted anything satisfactory for months. His first exhibitions, some ten years before, had been promising. He had soon become well-known in the south-east of England, and if his name was rarely mentioned in London art galleries, he was generally considered as a good painter with a sense of originality. There was, above all, one thing everyone agreed about: his imagination had no limits!

It had been the case until the source suddenly ran out. His loss of inspiration had corresponded with the period when the relationship with his female companion had begun to go wrong. She had started to reproach him with spending too much time with his children who moreover had great difficulty to accept her presence next to their father. Eventually he had made a choice, which had not been so simple, but by no means he would have sacrificed his daughter and son. He had broken up. Such an act had not been without any consequence. She had tried to make his life a hell. That, in a way, had made the break-up easier for him. The character she had revealed under the circumstance had confirmed his decision; yet it seemed that she had taken away from him every spark of imagination. He was like a lion in a cage, deprived of his instinct for creation.

Every time he started a new painting, he disliked it almost immediately. His art had become mere rubbish.

He suddenly stopped walking and began to search for a number in his phone book. He picked up the receiver and dialled a number. He waited.

"Hello!" a woman's voice answered.

"Hello, Charlotte! William speaking."

"William? What a surprise! How are you?"

"Well, it's a long story. What about you?"

"A long story, too."

He started telling her all about his own misfortune; the breaking-up, his artistic void, his loneliness. Charlotte was a lady about his age he had known for a long time and they were close enough to tell each other about their lives. He learnt that she had left her boyfriend; such a happy coincidence encouraged him to propose that they should meet soon. She accepted with a great deal of enthusiasm.

They actually met in front of the Osborne Studio Gallery, in Belgravia, on the following Saturday afternoon.

"Will, I'm so happy to see you again."

"So am I. Shall we go in?"

"With pleasure."

"These paintings are so sad," Charlotte said, after watching a few of them. William knew the artist who exhibited them, an obscure art teacher who hardly spoke to anybody outside his classroom. His name was Harry Smith.

"He has never painted anything funny," he answered.

"It makes me feel down!"

"Harry himself can make you feel down if you spend more than ten minutes in his company. He is quite successful yet; people like his paintings."

"Does he always paint ugly naked bodies?"

"He always paints naked people. His aim is not to paint Barbies, you know, but I must admit I don't like these bodies either."

They watched other styles of paintings around the gallery. Charlotte enjoyed some landscapes whereas William was more attracted by some abstract works. They left after half an hour and decided to have a drink.

"Let's go to the Paxton's Head, in Knightsbridge", he said. "Have you been there?"

"Never."

"It's quite nice, you know."

"It'll be O.K."

The pub wasn't very busy yet. Only a few customers were standing at the bar, and two young ladies were sitting at a table, chatting.

"Where shall we sit?" William asked.

Charlotte had a look around.

"Let's sit over there, on this wall seat. Do you mind?"

"That's perfect, Charlotte. Please make yourself comfortable. I'll have a pint of bitter. What about you?"

"What sort of bitter do they have here?"

"London Pride..."

"Great! Half a pint, please."

William ordered, and brought back the pint and a half of London Pride.

"So, you don't paint at the moment", Charlotte

said, "What a shame!"

"I'm not feeling like painting, you know; since Beverley and I parted, I've been idle. I'm not nostalgic about my relationship. It used to be great, I mean a long time ago, but I no longer miss her; it's just that I'm feeling lonely."

"I can understand that. It's the way I feel too. I put an end to my relation with Jeff; I had to, but I find it so hard to live alone."

"I'm lucky, in a way, because I have Julia and Marcus. As you have no children, it must be difficult."

"I really hoped Jeff and I would have kids. I'm thirty, so it wasn't too late for me, but he is such a drunkard!"

"Is he?"

"Definitely. When we met, two years ago, he was sober. He had just been through a detoxification programme. What a nice man he was! So gentle, so joyful, so funny, he really took care of me! And I know he really loves me!"

"A relapse?"

"Unfortunately. He hadn't drunk a drop of alcohol for a year and a half. We had spent wonderful holidays in Cyprus, and we clearly thought about living under the same roof when he started again. So far, we had lived separately, but he spent a lot of time with me, in my flat. One afternoon, I went to see him unexpectedly. I was just feeling like seeing him, and I found him half-drunk!"

"You must have been so disappointed!"

"Well, he claimed that it was an 'accident' and

promised he wouldn't do it again, but he was unable to keep his promise. I did my best to help him after a second detoxification programme. This time, he relapsed into drinking after six months. I couldn't stand going out with an alcoholic, a man who was drunk every day. So I decided to break up.

"You probably did the only thing you could do."

"Probably, but I feel selfish about that."

"You don't have to. With people like him, it never stops. Does he have a job?"

"Yes. He is a university teacher."

"So he's been fortunate enough not to lose his job!"

"I don't know how he manages to teach. His students have never complained."

"He must be brilliant!"

"He actually is. I would say he has all the qualities I could expect from a man. Unfortunately alcohol has made him a wreck!"

"How old is he?"

"He's thirty-eight. He used to be married, but his wife asked for a divorce after eight years. She was fed up."

"Gosh! That's a sad story. His sentimental life has already been broken twice because he likes his drink too much. How could he waste a love story with a woman like you? It's incredible! If I were him, I would have made another choice."

"I think he didn't choose."

"You feel sympathy for him, don't you? Do you still love him?"

"I don't know, and I no longer want to think about it."

"Good for you. You must protect yourself."

"What about you? How long did you stay with Beverley?"

"Almost three years."

"You told me about her dreadful behaviour. What did she do?"

"When I told her our love was over, she didn't accept my decision."

"She was partly responsible, wasn't she?"

"She was, but she wouldn't acknowledge that she had been too far, that she had been too demanding as far as my children had been concerned. So she did her best to destroy our good memories. For instance, she tore some photos we had taken during our trips abroad into pieces, then she sent them to me in a big envelope."

"What did she expect from that? Apart from spoiling your relation even more!"

"She had become sort of hysterical. When I went to ask her for some personals I had left in her house, she just wouldn't let me in."

"Was there anything valuable?"

"Some clothes, a few books about art I desperately wanted to get back, tools I used to do odd jobs with such as a hammer, a few wrenches, a carpenter's saw, a hand drill..."

"... Did she keep them all?"

"Worse than that. The next morning, I found everything on the pavement, in front of my garage door, except the tools she had used to make a real mess. She also massacred the objects I was most fond of; an easel, a sketch box and several paintings, and my guitar. I was furious!"

"What did you do?"

"There was nothing I could do. Lodge a complaint? I had no evidence, and it would have been easy for her to say that she had never seen any of these objects in her own house."

"What a lousy trick!"

"She didn't content herself with spoiling things, you know! She kept hounding me! She called my parents and told them I had left her because I was homosexual. She knew that she would shock them claiming I had a boyfriend."

"I can't understand how somebody can do that. It proved a total lack of respect towards your parents and you!"

"You can't imagine, when you live with a person, when life goes fine, that one day she will try to harm you as if you were her greatest enemy. Now I'm disgusted and I wonder how I happened to have some close relationship with a woman like her!"

"Some people, you know, start having a destructive attitude as soon as things go the wrong way for them, and they just don't think of the others any more."

"Just like Jeff who didn't think of you when he started drinking again!"

"We both had relations with selfish people!"

"When you come and see me at home, I will show you a letter she wrote to the owner of a gallery in which I was to exhibit my paintings."

"A letter?"

"I haven't told you the whole story yet!"

They agreed that Charlotte would come for dinner the next Friday. As if by magic, William felt a desire for creating again. Back home, he took out his brushes, tubes of paint, easel and canvas, and spent the following days in his studio. When Friday evening came, he displayed to Charlotte the three paintings he had made. One of them, which was untitled, was Kandinsky-like. She enjoyed it, but she preferred the second one, called 'Red Dream', full of happiness and bright colours. On the contrary, she disliked the third one, 'Something Dark", because it was obscure, sad and dismal.

"I love the first two, but this one makes me feel ill-at-ease", she said, "Were you in a bad mood when you painted it?"

"I was thinking of the ravens of my childhood. They were flying in big circles above my head. Their croaking in the Autumn mist sounded in my chest like the bang of hunting guns. I hated them."

Charlotte looked both puzzled and moved.

"Sometimes, when I was very young, it seemed to me that their dance in the sky was like a macabre ceremony. Their screams sounded infernal, and I felt in jeopardy. I imagined that one of them would land and change into a tall man wearing black clothes and a devilish mask, then he would walk in my direction, laughing nastily, until we came face to face. Paralyzed as I was, I almost saw the frightening creature pointing a long sharp-nailed finger at me. I started running back to the farmhouse. I didn't stop until I had reached the door I banged close behind me. I entered my bedroom hastily, jumped into bed and hid under the cover. I could remain motionless for hours. I didn't listen to my mother who was trying to reassure me. I only came out when I heard my father's voice; I felt protected then.

"What an amazing story!"

"I know. In fact, ravens have never harmed me, except in my imagination. Shall we have dinner?"

"With great pleasure."

They talked about people they had both known in the past, then William asked about Jeff.

"I had some news during the week. He called me, as he does regularly. He wasn't feeling well, as usual."

"Still drinking?"

"He always swears he has stopped, but I'm sure he still drinks. I can hear that."

"I'm sorry for you. I know this isn't my business, but don't you think he should stop calling you?"

"You must be right, but it's difficult to refuse to answer him. He's feeling bad."

"Yet he should take responsibility for himself. You won't be free as long as he remains a burden for you."

"I know that. I just think that I can't let him down. By the way, you intend to show me a letter, don't you?"

"Yes, indeed. Let me fetch it."

He came back after a short while.

"Here it is. The director of a famous gallery in London had agreed about a two-month exhibition of thirty paintings. It was a great opportunity for me because I had financial difficulties at that time. So, Beverley sent this to him."

William handed the letter to Charlotte. She read it in a low voice:

Mr William Ward
36, Cleveland Street
City of Westminster
London, W1T

September 3ʳᵈ, 2005

Sir,

Let me tell you that the exhibition we have scheduled, which is to open to the public next Friday, will by no means be presented.

What I have recently heard about you concerning your unfair business dealings with various artists, your foul attitude towards them, has led me to cancel this exhibition. One of them even told me you were a stupid motherfucker, which I am inclined to believe.

Needless to say that I will do my best to damage your good name !

W. Ward

"How dared she write such ravings on your behalf?"
"She suddenly had no limit as far as revenge was

concerned. I think she desperately tried to destroy me."

"What about the exhibition then?"

"You must imagine how astonished I was when I received a letter from the gallery which let me know that I wouldn't be welcome any more in London artistic circles. I drove there straight away, but the director refused to see me. His personal assistant gave me this copy of the letter.

"Did you try to explain the situation to her?"

"I did; she wouldn't listen."

"It wasn't your fault though."

"I tried to say that Beverley had typed the letter and imitated my signature, but it was useless. I tried to get in touch with the director several times afterwards, without success."

"And you couldn't prove that Beverley had written and sent it, I suppose."

"I'm almost sure she didn't even use her own computer. She must have been to a cybercafé. Fortunately I still had access to a few galleries in the South, and I managed to sell a few paintings in Paris, thanks to a friend."

"Anyway you seem to feel inspired again. You'll go on painting, won't you? You no longer need a muse !"

"Let's say I may have found a new one!"

"Really?"

"And you may be this one!"

"Am I?"

"I think you are!"

They had been lovers for about six months when they visited Paris and Honfleur together, during the second fortnight of June. Charlotte had got into the habit of spending several nights a week at William's place. Back to London, she carried on this way. Yet, one evening, she phoned to tell him she couldn't come.

"We are supposed to go to the cinema", he answered.

"I know, but a colleague of mine is having trouble with her son who has run away from home."

"How old is he?"

"He's twelve. She's awfully worried, so I proposed to spend the evening with her. I might stay very late, perhaps the whole night."

"I understand. Let me know if, by chance, her son comes back soon. We might go to the half past ten showing then."

"Perhaps, but I can't promise. I'll see you tomorrow anyway. I must go now. Have a nice evening."

"All right. Bye, Charlotte."

"Bye, Will."

She didn't call him again that night. He tried to concentrate on a painting he had started in the afternoon. At three o'clock in the morning, he went to bed, little satisfied with his work, and had some difficulty to fall asleep. He was worried about Charlotte, although he didn't know why. It was just a strange feeling. He missed her.

He woke up at dawn, feeling tired. He prepared some toast with jam he wasn't in the right mood to eat. After having a quick cup of coffee, he unsuccessfully tried to paint again. He stood in front of the canvas for about ten minutes, brush in hand. His mind focused on Charlotte. Even though he had no reason for not believing her, he was feeling restless. Every day some kids probably ran away from home; most of them came back after wandering in the streets for a few hours. Others took the train for another town, searching for adventure, but they soon felt homesick. Sometimes they were spotted by a police patrol and driven back to mum and dad. There was nothing unbelievable about such a story; this was at least what William was trying to convince himself of. He had a second cup of coffee, then a third one, before going for an early morning walk. It was still cool outside, but the streets were kind of hostile. He felt like an alien who had just got out of his flying saucer, lost in a world he wasn't meant to live in. He paid no attention to the passers-by he met. 'I'm happy with Charlotte', he thought; 'she's a marvellous woman and we get on wonderfully, don't we? So, what's going wrong?' As he found no answer to this question, he decided to visit her. It would be better than ringing up and he would be O.K. as soon as he could see her. He drove to Bedford Gardens, next to Holland Park, and stopped his car about fifty yards away from her house. He was about to get out when he saw a man going through the front gate into the street. He was quite tall, grey-haired, with black jeans and a short-sleeved white shirt on. He knew instinctively it was Jeff although he had never met him before.

William remained motionless for a few minutes. How could that be? 'They have spent the night together. She lied to me last night. The kid hasn't stirred from home. He was probably watching TV or playing some computer game. What a fool I have been!' When he finally got out of his car, Jeff had disappeared. 'Be quiet, Will! Perhaps it's just a coincidence. Charlotte probably came back from her friend's in the middle of the night and he visited her this morning. He may have stayed only a few minutes. She must have sent him off!'

He crossed the front garden and rang the bell.

"Anything wrong, Jeff?" She opened the door. "Oh, Wil ! I..."

"You didn't expect me, did you? It seems as if you were expecting to see someone else!"

"I wasn't expecting anybody's visit. What a surprise! Are you all right, Will?"

"I don't know, actually. What about the runaway kid?"

"The runaway kid? Oh... He came back to his mum's. It was over midnight when he turned up!"

"That's good news."

"It is indeed... I went to bed late, you know, so I'm still half asleep this morning. I was about to call you."

"I'm sure you were."

"Come on, Will. Please sit down. You look strange, don't you?"

"It's just because I heard someone else's name when I rang!"

"Oh, don't worry, Will. I said 'Jeff' because he had just left."

"I actually saw him as he was leaving. I was quite amazed."

"I understand. He just came to speak."

"He could have called you."

"Of course, but... He didn't stay more than... half an hour or so."

William didn't know if he was feeling better or worse. On the one hand, he had good reasons for being reassured; on the other hand, he remembered that she had received some messages during their stay in France. She didn't look at them at once. 'It can't be important', she kept saying. Once, as he was coming out of the bathroom, he had seen her on the phone. She had hung up immediately.

"How did you know it was Jeff?" she asked in order to interrupt a situation which had turned to be quite embarrassing.

"Intuition."

"Ah?" That was all she had managed to answer. She had to say something else not to be faced with questions.

"You don't have to worry", she continued, 'I understand perfectly that you may be upset, but he just came, so I let him in. I just tried not to be mean. I would have told you, anyway."

She sat astride on his knees and looked at him straight in the eye.

"Oh, Will!" she said, holding his face in her hands.

He smiled and hugged her in a long embrace. They made love on the sofa, then they went to the Anchor, on the south bank of the Thames, where they had lunch outside.

They were sitting at a table next to a young couple who were having sandwiches and pints of

London Pride. They were talking about some kind of business in relation with life insurance. The man expressed himself quietly whereas his wife constantly spoke with her hands. He took his eyes off her to stare at the content of Charlotte's plate for a while, then he seemed to take interest in the red window frames of the Anchor. William was observing the people who were passing between the pub and its outside tables; a muscular young man, stripped to the waist, roller-skating, groups of tourists strolling along towards the Millennium Bridge and the Tate Modern, others going the opposite way towards City Hall. He turned his head to look at 30, St Mary Axe, on the north bank. In the meantime the woman had gone to the toilets.

"Do you like the Gherkin?" her husband asked him, "It makes me think of what my dear wife never thinks about! She's always talking about her job!"

"Well, Charlotte can make love while talking about work; you should try!"

The young man didn't know what to answer.

'And maybe she can have sex with two men on the same day', William thought.

"Are you sulking?" he asked Charlotte after the couple had left.

"Charlotte can make love while talking about work! You've been rude to me. I was so embarrassed!"

"Come on, I was only joking!"

"You've made a fool of me! What does this bloke think of me now?"

"Why the hell do you care about what he thinks of you? We had never met him before and we'll probably never see him again. He's a complete unknown!"

"It wasn't a way of treating me, that's all!"

"I'm sorry, Charlotte. Let's say it was a bad joke."

"A very bad one indeed. Do you mind leaving now? I'd like to have a walk."

"O.K. Which way would you like to go?"

"Let's go to Tower Bridge, then we'll cross and get to the City."

"As you like!"

They had a nice time walking although Charlotte was still a little tense.

"Why haven't you painted it yet?" she asked him when they arrived at the foot of the Gherkin.

"I don't know. I guess I have never thought about painting it."

"You should. I suggest you might show it as a gigantic sex with a swarm of naked women around trying to have a bit of it."

"I might as well draw a horde of naked Charlottes around the Gherkin, so that it would become The Big Sex, just as New York has become The Big Apple!"

"Don't even think about it!"

"It doesn't sound like a bad idea. Let me think about it!"

He looked at her in a malicious way.

"What?" she asked.

"Nothing. I was just pulling your leg!"

"Good for you!"

They started laughing.

"It's a pity", he continued. " It could have been a great painting!"

"Just do it, I'll kill you!"

"That won't be necessary", he answered, thinking sadly that this enormous phallus might in fact be Jeff's. He realized that his suspicion of Charlotte's relationship with that man was becoming an obsession he had to get rid of straight away.

When they reached the Monument, Charlotte suggested that they went to the top. "The view of London is nice from up there", she declared.

"I guess so."

They climbed up the narrow staircase of three hundred and eleven steps.

Once in the cage added in the mid-nineteenth century to prevent people from jumping off, he asked her if she knew why it is two hundred and two feet high.

"I don't know."

"As a matter of fact, it is positioned two hundred and two feet from the spot in Pudding Lane on which the Great Fire of London started in 1666."

"Well done, Mr Christopher Wren!"

"I must admit it's a little too high for me."

"Are you feeling dizzy?"

"Not really, but..."

He saw, down there in the street, a man wearing black jeans and a short-sleeved white shirt who was looking up in their direction. He was quite tall and grey-haired, and seemed to stare at him as if to tell him 'I'm here, boy, I'm still here!'

"What's going on, Will?"

"Nothing, really. Don't worry."

"Come on, let's go down."

"I'm all right. Let's stay for a while."

The man in the street had disappeared. Yet William was almost sure he had just seen Jeff again.

In the evening, as they were taking a breath of fresh air, he thought about the event again then he concluded that he had hallucinated and promised to himself he would forget it.

"What about some croissants for breakfast?" he asked Charlotte when they woke up the next morning.

"Wonderful idea!"

"All right. I'll have a shower, then I'll go straight to the baker's."

"You needn't do it, you know. We might just stay in bed for a while and have some toast."

"No. We'll have some nice French croissants."

"Very nice of you. Let me give you a French kiss then. You deserve it."

Contrary to the previous morning, he was walking with a big smile on his face; the people he met were his friends and the baker's shop was the promised land although the very young lady who served him had chocolate spots on her white baby-T, as if out of tune in a world of harmony. He wasn't affected by this. On the way back he was almost running, impatient as he was to have breakfast in the garden with Charlotte.

He was about two hundred yards from his house when he saw a man whose silhouette now looked familiar to him ringing the bell, which made his blood boil at once. He started running with the intention of crossing the street, which he was prevented from by a lorry. When he finally set foot on the opposite pavement, there was nobody. He couldn't have vanished in the air! 'She let him in', he thought, 'I can't believe it!'

He rushed into the bedroom, panting.

"Where is he?"

Charlotte sat up and stared wide-eyed.

"Who?"

"You know who I mean!"

"Will, there's nobody here!"

"I saw him enter the house!"

"A burglar?"

"What do you mean? Was it a burglar I saw at Bedford Gardens yesterday morning?"

"Oh, stop it, please!"

"Tell him to stop it! Tell him!"

"Are you getting mad?"

"I saw him!"

"You can't have seen him!"

"He was in the street!"

"He must be home at this time, like you and me. Do you want me to call him? Will you be satisfied then?"

"Don't do it. I must be mistaken. I must have seen some fellow who looks like him and... Well, I'm sorry."

He sat on the bed and looked at her sadly.

"I must be crazy!"

"Please forget about it. Let's have a nice breakfast, then we might spend the weekend in Plymouth. I have a friend there who's going to Belgium for a couple of days. When she comes to London, she often puts up at me. Would you like me to ask her if we can go there?"

"It would do me good."

"I'll call her then.

They were in Plymouth by the end of the afternoon. Helen, Charlotte's friend, was there to welcome them before driving to Dover harbour. William saw no ghost on the beach, no man looking like Jeff in the streets or in shops. Yet, on Saturday, he surprised her on the phone in the kitchen. Like in France, she hung up as soon as he entered. In the evening, as she was having a shower, he yielded to temptation and searched in her cellphone memory who she had called. Whereas he expected to find a hidden number, he was surprised to read 'Georgina – 13.44'. Feeling stupid and guilty, he put the phone back and promised to himself never to spy on her again.

He felt much more relaxed from then on. They returned to London on Sunday evening. Charlotte left for Bedford Gardens on Monday, early in the afternoon, and came back before dinner. He had started a new painting representing a summer scene on a Devon beach, which he finished two days later.

He went to bed late on Tuesday evening ; Charlotte was asleep. In the middle of the night, he woke up all of a sudden, sweating. He felt completely lost for a couple of seconds, then he remembered that in his nightmare, he was going through Leicester Square with Charlotte when a man took her by the hand and dragged her off. He wanted to run after them but the fog surrounded him. It was so thick that he couldn't see anyone or anything. When it cleared away at last, they had disappeared.   Later he found himself standing at the foot of the Monument. Looking up, he saw them waving to him, both smiling. He hurried to the top. When he reached it, completely out of breath, he was alone. London had vanished under the fog again. He heard them laughing in the distance.

William recollected the story bit by bit. It ended at the Anchor; this time, it was Jeff who was asking him "Do you like the Gherkin?", adding "Charlotte loves it. She calls it 'The Big Sex'! She's so excited every time we come here!"

"I hate the fucking Gherkin", he answered.

Jeff burst out laughing and took charlotte in his arms. Just as William was rushing him, they disappeared once again, then it was all over.

As time was passing by, William was feeling worse and worse. Several times a week he was subject to hallucinations and made awful dreams. Sleepless nights exhausted him. He couldn't help thinking that the relationship between Jeff and Charlotte wasn't over. She was nice to him yet, so he felt reassured as long as they were together, but negative thinking came to his mind when they parted for a few hours or a whole night. In her absence he spent his time painting nightmarish scenes. His style had become tormented. Once he drew the Gherkin with Charlotte sitting at the top, waiting, as the prize promised to the winner. Behind her, a gigantic, frightening coarse-featured character was stretching out his hand to capture her. From then on, his paintings became more and more terrifying. 'I'm getting mad', he said to himself one day, as he was about to enter his study. 'I mustn't go in.' He turned back and hurried out of his house. He ran to the nearest underground station and took the tube for Trafalgar Square, then he spent the whole afternoon at the National Gallery.

As he was coming out, he saw a man standing at the bottom of the steps. He was watching Nelson's Column absent-mindedly. 'I must be dreaming again', he thought. He went down to him and watched his face. He was real, badly-shaved, looking tired; he had nothing to attract Charlotte. How could she still have a love affair with such a wretched fellow? He looked like a drunkard.

"Lots of people today!" William said.

He got no answer.

"Do you live in London?" he asked.

The man didn't seem to hear him.

"Are you Jeff?"

His interlocutor suddenly stared at him.

"It's my name! Who are you?"

"My name's William."

"William?"

"I would like to talk to you about Charlotte."

"Why?"

"Is she your lover?"

"I suppose you're pulling my leg! What a motherfucker you are!"

"You know who I am, don't you?"

"More or less."

"What do you mean?"

"I just know you're the son-of-a-bitch she fell in love with after dumping me. Leave me alone!"

"How stupid I have been! I'm convinced now!"

"What are you convinced of?"

"Blimey! When I think that I worried myself sick for weeks! I'm suddenly feeling so well! Thanks ever so much. I'll say hello to Charlotte for you, I promise."

"Piss off!"

William decided to walk home. He certainly wouldn't tell Charlotte about this meeting. He wouldn't mention Jeff. He was half way through when his cellphone rang.

"Hello!"

"Hello, dear. Are you O.K.?"

"I'm fine. I hadn't been feeling so well for ages."

"Good news! That's great!"

"What time will you turn up?"

"Within an hour or so."

"All right. I'll start preparing dinner soon. What about some Champagne?"

"Champagne? Shall we be celebrating something special?"

"Yes. We'll drink to our love and happiness!"

"It sounds wonderful. I'm looking forward to it... Well, I've got to hang up. I can't hear you very well with all that noise around Piccadilly Circus. I'm going to Trafalgar Square; it will be more peaceful there."

"Trafalgar Square?"

"Sorry?"

"What will you do at Trafalgar Square?"

"Oh, I will stay there for a while before taking the tube. I love it with all those tourists who speak all sorts of foreign languages. See you later, Will. Bye."

"Bye."

When Charlotte entered the living-room, she found William despondent. She was all the more in a state of amazement that he had been so enthusiastic on the phone.

"Ready for Champagne?" she asked, pretending to ignore his conspicuous change of mood.

"Why did you go to Trafalgar Square?" she heard as an answer.

"What's the matter about Trafalgar Square? I like going there from time to time."

"Who did you meet there?"

"Admiral Nelson! He chatted me up a little! Very nice fellow, actually. The lions didn't eat me, and I met the Queen who invited me for dinner at Buckingham Palace; after weighing up the pros and cons, I decided to refuse. Just to spend the evening with you!"

"I'm not such a fool as you make me!" he said, rising to his feet. "You were not alone at Trafalgar Square!"

"Of course I wasn't, I've just told you!" she shouted.

"You were with him, once again. I saw him there. So you're trapped, you bitch!"

"So I'm a bitch! This is the first time you've insulted me! And it will be the last one! I'm fed up with your stupid jealousy! I've been patient, but the cup is full now!"

She went out at once, slamming the door.

"Go to hell", William said after she had left. He felt so unhappy! 'I'm just a fool, a poor damn fool who's just driven his lover away! I must do something to be forgiven. I'll go and see her at once, then I'll take her to the restaurant.'

He was coldly welcome at Bedford Gardens. Although he apologized, Charlotte didn't let him in at first. She eventually accepted his invitation but she insisted upon being given a lift home after dinner.

"Why don't you come and sleep with me?" he tried once more, just before she got out of his car.

"Will, please, leave me alone now. You must understand you've upset me. I can't accept being insulted like that."

"I can understand that I've been a bit too far, but you must admit I can hardly believe in such a coincidence."

"You don't trust me, do you?"

"I'm afraid I can't."

"Good night, Will."

"Good night."

He felt angry now. Whereas he had been afraid of losing her, he was no longer scared and he didn't really know why. Oddly enough, he slept like a log and woke up late on the morrow. He decided to leave for a few days. He would visit Ray, a friend of his who lived in a cottage in Salisbury. He wouldn't call Charlotte and didn't expect any news from her. Yet she phoned him in the evening. She sounded panicky, completely lost. He promised to visit her as soon as he was back.

Two days later, he was in London again. He had missed Charlotte even if he had been in good company with Ray and his girlfriend. Visiting Wookey Hole Caves had been relaxing and he had enjoyed walking in the nearby forest. Nevertheless he was looking forward to seeing her again; a mutual feeling, according to the messages she had sent to him.

He was about to leave for Charlotte's when someone knocked at the door. He opened and saw Jeff standing in front of him.

"Hello, will you let me in? I have something to tell you."

"Why should I? Why do you want to speak to a motherfucker like me?"

"Because Charlotte and I are still lovers!"

William couldn't believe his ears.

"Are you? I suppose you're pulling my leg!"

"I'm afraid I'm not."

"All right. Come in and tell me about you two. It might be funny!"

"I don't think there's anything funny."

"Sit down. You will probably understand if I don't offer you anything to drink, won't you?"

"This won't be necessary."

"O.K. I'm listening to you."

"Well, when you started your love affair with Charlotte, we had broken up."

"I already know that."

"What you may not know is that we started our relation again about two months later. We both had understood we were still in love with each other. The problem is..."

"Please go on."

"You!"

"Me? Charlotte loves me and I love her! I think the problem is that you can't accept this fact."

"She just doesn't want to hurt you. She's a

sensitive one, you know."

"How dare you? What a fucking son-of-a-bitch you are!"

William got up and hurried to the door to open it.

"Go away from here!" he yelled. "Don't ever come back!"

"O.K. but I don't think this is the best way to solve the problem."

"That's enough. Get out of here!"

"So you don't believe me!"

"I don't."

"Why don't you call Charlotte then? Ask her to come over here, so that we could speak together? You'd know I'm not lying!"

"Go to hell!"

Jeff didn't push the matter any further. William felt nervous after he had left. He couldn't believe that man had come to see him to suggest such a confrontation. His attitude was ever so insulting. Yet he couldn't but think that he could possibly have told the truth. Was he a maniac, a manipulator, or just a jealous man?

An hour later, Charlotte was falling into his arms.

"I missed you so much, darling. I'm so happy."

"So am I."

They had hardly had time to kiss each other when the doorbell rang. It was Jeff again. He had been following William to Bedford Gardens.

"Jeff! What are you doing here?"

"I'm here because I love you!"

"You can't stay, Jeff!"

"Why can't I stay whereas he can?"

He pushed the door open and went into the living-room.

"Hello, nice to see you again, Will!"

"I'm fed up with you! Charlotte, that guy visited me just before I came here. Did you follow me?"

"I actually did. Now we can talk at last!"

"No way. Kick him out!"

"You must go now", Charlotte said.

"I want to talk. Now tell him we're still together."

"Jeff, stop making a fuss!"

"Just tell him I was waiting for you at Trafalgar Square."

"Stop it!" she shouted.

"Tell him we see each other several times a week..."

William looked at Charlotte in wonder.

"... We sleep together every Tuesday night; and what about yesterday, and last night?"

She sat in the sofa and began to cry.

"Charlotte", William said, "He isn't telling the truth, is he?"

She remained silent.

"Please tell me that's all lies!"

"I'm sorry, Will", she answered. "I love you. I'm so sorry!"

"Do you love him?"

"He's telling the truth."

"Do you love him?" he asked again.

"Well... I..."

William looked at Jeff. The blood rushed to his head. He was feeling like smashing his face. He looked at Charlotte; they both looked miserable.

"Charlotte, you've fooled me. I had doubts about you and him, and I was right; I wasn't mad!"

"Will, let me..."

"No, Charlotte. It would be useless."

"Don't worry, my dear love. I will look after you", he heard as he was leaving. 'They really deserve each other!' he thought.

He was coming out of the baker's, the next morning, when a young man who was waiting for the bus greeted him.

"Hello!" he said, smiling.

He was in his early twenties, dressed in almost worn-out, poor quality clothes. He looked excited.

"Hello!" William answered.

"Hey, look!"

He pointed his finger towards the church, opposite the street.

"Have you seen him?"

"Who?"

"Look! It's John! ... John Lennon!"

The young man looked happy; a broad smile illuminated his face.

"You're right. It must be John Lennon."

"So you can see him! You can see him!"

William wondered if he had said the right thing.

"I'm Paul. I'm so glad to have a new friend!"

"Well, my name is William. As a matter of fact, I'm not sure this man is John Lennon. I'm not even sure there is anybody in front of the church."

Paul frowned.

"It's because he's gone. But he was there! You've seen him, haven't you?"

"Well... I think so."

Paul was smiling again.

"Have a nice day, Paul!"

"Have a nice day, William! Will you come to our concert tonight?"

"Your concert?"

"Yeah. I'll be at Wembley Stadium with John, Ringo and George!"

"All right. See you tonight then!"

DESPERATE FOR LOVE

John Drummond had just left his estate agency. Like every evening, he had been working late. He wouldn't be home before ten, which didn't really matter as nobody was expecting him. He would have a quick dinner, as usual; some ready-made course from Tesco's frozen food department, or some sliced ham with red beans, and a flavoured yoghurt. After making sure his former wife had sent no urgent message concerning their ten-year-old daughter he was to welcome at the weekend, he would connect to the internet.

Harry, a friend of his who worked as a banker, had advised him to register on a dating and chatting site.

"Don't stay alone. You must have some opportunities to meet some nice women at work."

"Not really. My colleague and my secretary are both married, and they aren't really attractive anyway."

"What about your clients?"

"They are just clients."

"Why don't you try the web, then?"

"The internet?"

"Definitely. I myself registered a fortnight ago, and I have a date on Saturday. A lovely blonde from Brighton! It's easy and it works ever so well. You just have to pay about twenty pounds a month and sit in front of your computer screen and chat."

"No, I wouldn't like that. It's not natural, I mean... It isn't my cup of tea."

"How do you know? Just try before saying 'no'. You're always complaining because you have no time to go out. Thanks to those sites, you can just stay at home and have fun, and meet somebody nice."

"I'll think about it."

John had actually thought it over and had concluded that the idea didn't sound so stupid, after all. He would try his luck tonight.

He connected to a site whose first page consisted in filling in a registry form. To start with, he had to create a username and a password.

'JohnnyD', he thought, 'that would be fine. Let's try it.'

Unfortunately it wasn't accepted. 'Your username is already taken! You must change it or choose another from the following list', he read. He was given the choice between 'JohnnyD-a-622', 'JohnnyD-a-104', 'JohnnyD-a-568' and 'JohnnyD-a-250'. He found those names rather complicated and hard to remember, so he searched for another one. Indeed, 'JohnD' didn't prove to be better, 'JohnLondon' was refused, but 'Jdrum' was alright. Second step, the password. This time it happened to be easier as 'DrumJohn' was original enough not to have been taken before. Then he entered his email address, 'jdrummond@tiscali.co.uk', supposed to be 'confidential, required in order to receive information concerning your account', and ticked 'I am a man seeking a woman, between 25 and 45, I was born on April 12th, 1971, my country of residence is the United Kingdom, I certify that I am over 18 and have read the Terms and Conditions as well as the privacy policy.'

The following step consisted in giving 'Your personal information':

Your marital status: divorced.

Do you have children? 1.

Your height: 6"0".

Your build: .....

The choice John was given seemed quite odd to him. 'Muscular' could impress some women though not most of them; 'average/medium', far too common, wouldn't sound very attractive; 'on the larger side' didn't match him; as for 'curvaceous' and 'slim', he actually was half way between both, so he answered 'slim', which was undoubtedly more flattering.

Your hair colour: dark brown.

Colour of your eyes: green.

John had to click on 'Register and continue' before filling in the next part of the form. He had then completed ten per cent of his own profile.

You live: alone.

Do you want other children? No.

Your nationality: British.

Foreign languages spoken: (2 possible choices) : French and Spanish.

Your religion: Atheist.

Your profession: Executive.

Your education level: university of life.

Your income: I'd rather not say.

Your relationship: a casual relationship.

Once again, clicking on 'Register and continue' was required. John's profile was now completed up to thirty per cent. He then filled in 'Your physical description' and 'Your character':

Your weight: 11st 2lb.

Your hair: short.

Your ethnicity: Caucasian/White.

How would you describe your physical appearance? .....

The registering members only had three possibilities. 'Very attractive' was tempting, but many a woman would be sceptical; 'average' was out of question, so 'attractive' appeared to be the only sensible choice to make.

Your style: classical.

Your most attractive aspect: my smile.

Your most distinguished character trait: easy-going.

Are you romantic? .....

'Very romantic' was definitely out of reach for a man who was seeking casual relationship. Being 'not romantic at all' would mean he only wanted sex, 'not very romantic' sounded hardly better, so he ticked 'romantic'.

You think marriage is: not necessary.

Next to 'Register and continue', which he was fed up with, he read 'I'll do this later – Show me who's online now!', which he clicked on. He had access to various women's profiles and was invited to write his 'personal ad'. This was to be thought of carefully; it had to be catchy enough to arouse curiosity without sounding pretentious.

'Let's take the plunge, John', he said to himself, and he started writing his ad.

'Hello! I'm a thirty-eight year-old divorced man. I am an estate agent in London. It's the first time I have been on this kind of site, so I don't really know what to say except that I like arts, reading, playing tennis when I have time enough, and I have fallen in love with France where I regularly spend my summer holidays because I enjoy the culture and way of life there.

I would like to meet people who are up for having fun, eating out, travelling, so if you are an active person, I think we will get on well. I equally appreciate sitting in a pub for a drink and a nice evening talk.

Well, if you have got this far and haven't had a nervous breakdown, maybe you would like to know more. Please simply ask! I'm looking forward to hearing from you.

Jdrum'

He 'submitted his ad', used his credit card to pay for a three-month subscription and logged off, satisfied. Just like Harry, he might soon meet a splendid creature. One weekend out of two, when he wasn't in charge of welcoming Sarah, he would be busy with a new conquest. He felt great under the shower and, once in bed, he started thinking of all those women who didn't even know yet how lucky they were. The web lover they had desperately expected for ages had registered at last!

The next day, he was busy at the agency in the morning. He thought about logging in but he couldn't do so in the presence of Joan, his secretary.

Jessie and Michael, his two colleagues, were out. He spent the afternoon showing potential buyers round some flats. He connected to the internet at last in the evening; he was immediately invited to 'bring his profile to life' by publishing his photo. He searched on his computer but didn't find a good one. On second thoughts, although it was said that 'profiles with photos are contacted 10 times more frequently than those without', he considered it was unreasonable to show his picture to everyone.

Time had come for him to have a look at some ladies' profiles. He started to 'wink at' those who lived in London. A few of them being online, he sent messages. It took at least fifteen minutes before he received an answer from Lolita 9854, which consisted in "Hello, how are you?" "Fine", John replied, adding that it would be nice if they chatted in order to know a little more about each other. The "Of course" he got in return made him think there was nothing to gain from corresponding with her. All of a sudden he had simultaneous answers from Adriana 4663 and Emma 2977 who seemingly were much more likely to start some interesting conversation. Unfortunately they both logged off after half an hour, yet promising to send emails on the morrow. He felt somewhat disappointed, and called Harry the next morning.

"Hello, John. How are you?"

"Not too bad. I just wanted to tell you I registered on a dating site..."

"... Did you? That's fine, you're gonna have a lot of fun, you know."

"As a matter of fact I tried to chat last night, but I wasn't very successful. I didn't manage to have a real conversation with anybody."

"Relax! It was your first evening on the site, wasn't it?"

"It actually was."

"The women you got in touch with were just careful and wanted to know more before confiding in you. It's a good point that they didn't talk much. Just show them how sensitive you are!"

"How can I do that if we don't talk?"

"Be patient. Your time will come, boy. Answer their emails and log in tonight; it will be the beginning of the weekend, so they will have more time for chatting, but don't rush them; they would hate you for that."

"What about your date?"

"Tomorrow afternoon, guy! I'll have a hell of a great time with Melinda! Will you be with Sarah tomorrow?"

"Definitely. I'll stop working at noon, just like every Saturday, and she'll stay with me until Sunday evening."

"It won't prevent you from being on the internet at night, I suppose. If your luck's in, you may have a date for next weekend!"

"I hope so. Let's wait and see."

"I'll tell you about mine. I'll be in Manchester from Monday to Wednesday. I'll call you when I'm back."

"All right. Have a nice time then."

"Thanks, good luck. Bye."

"Bye."

At the end of his working day, he found no message from Emma 2977, but he had received two from women he had winked at, and two more from Adriana 4663. The three were online, so he started chatting with them. Monica 3616 and Ginger 7153 didn't prove to be very keen whereas Adriana, whose real name was Emily, showed a lot of curiosity about John. She soon became her only interlocutor and they conversed for almost two hours.

"... I'm 38. I work as an estate agent."

"I'm 34. I work as a personal assistant. Are you an employee or the boss?"

"I'm the boss. What sort of company do you work in?"

"An insurance company. Which London area do you work in?"

"Twickenham, and I live there, too."

While Emily was writing her answer, he had a quick look at her profile in order to check a few details: single, no children, 5 feet 7 inches, light brown hair, blue eyes, 9 stones 6 pounds, white, attractive, no foreign language spoken. It was flattering, just like everybody's.

"That's why you're fond of tennis then!"

"???"

"The famous tournament!"

"Do you mean 'Wimbledon tournament'? I'm afraid Twickenham is famous for rugby!"

"Oh, sorry, I always mistake Wimbledon for Twickenham!"

"Never mind. Where do you live?"

"I live in Enfield."

"What do you do at weekends? Read? Practise sport?"

"I read or visit friends. I practise gymnastics on Saturday mornings and I go swimming during the week. What about you? Do you read a lot?"

"When I have time. I've just read an interesting novel in French."

"Really? You're quite good at languages, aren't you? I'm not. Which book is it?"

"It's Alexandre Dumas's Madame Bovary. It's the story of Emma Bovary, a married woman abandoned by her two successive lovers, Rodolphe and Léon. Crippled with debt, she finally poisons herself with arsenic."

"Do you mean Gustave Flaubert's Madame Bovary?"

John felt ashamed. He had actually read the novel in French, yet a long time before.

"Of course. I'm sorry."

"Dumas Junior wrote the Lady of the Camellias! Have you read it?"

"No; I saw a film about it years ago. I don't remember the story."

"It deals with the life of Marguerite Gautier, a young beautiful courtesan in Paris, who is in a fragile physical state (she has tuberculosis). Armand Duval falls in love with her. At the end of the story, she is very ill and dies in his arms."

"Quite a moving story, isn't it?"

"It surely is. Do you like Emma Bovary?"

He was more and more embarrassed. Emily seemed to know much more about French literature than he actually did and he didn't want to disappoint her.

"She's quite romantic but she can't achieve her desires in the nineteenth century society. I really like her as a heroine."

"I agree with you."

As he hadn't done too badly, John considered it was time to change subjects.

"What sort of woman are you? I mean, are you particular about your appearance?"

"I would say I am. I like dressing up when I go to the restaurant, for instance. What about you? You're the classic style, aren't you?"

"Yes, I wear a suit and a tie every day at work. I like it and it's a way to show my clients that I respect them. Of course I like being well-dressed when I go to the restaurant or the theatre."

"Have you been to the theatre recently?"

"Unfortunately I haven't. Do you dress up only for eating out? What do you wear at work?"

"I don't like wearing strict clothes, except for important meetings. Would you like to go and watch a musical one day?"

"Why not? It sounds like a good idea."

"Have you seen 'Chicago'? The film, I mean."

"I've seen it."

"It's on in a theatre near Leicester Square. It's said to be good."

"Would you like to see it?"

"I would be delighted."

"What about talking about it on the phone, then?"

He knew she wouldn't answer positively at once,

and she didn't; so they carried on conversing for a while, until he suggested that she might call him."

"I'll give you my cellphone number. You don't have to give me yours. That sounds fair enough, doesn't it?"

"The last time I accepted this kind of proposal, I was insulted by the man who had given me his number."

"We'll have to speak anyway. We can't go and watch a musical without talking before."

"This is what we're doing, isn't it?"

"Would you rather meet me in a pub? It's up to you."

"All right. I prefer calling you."

"07726704847; I'm logging off. I'll be with you on the phone in a minute, if you call me."

"Don't worry, I will. I'm logging off as well."

'Well done,' John thought, a little fed up with chatting on the net, 'let's have a real conversation at last. I hope she has a beautiful voice.'

It was over midnight. He waited. Five minutes passed. She hadn't called yet. Maybe she wouldn't. He was wondering how Harry managed to have dates with wonderful women whereas it seemed to be so hard.

The telephone rang. He was sure her voice would match her physically. He knew it was often the case.

"Hello, Emily speaking. I'm sorry for keeping you waiting. I had some trouble getting through, but it's O.K. now."

She really had a soft and pleasant voice. 'She must be so attractive', he said to himself, 'how lucky I am!'

"Hello, Emily. It's nice to hear you. I must say it's much better to talk with you on the phone."

"Well... You would like to talk about 'Chicago', wouldn't you?"

"Yes, indeed. Would you mind watching it with me next Saturday night?"

"That would be great."

"Perfect. I'll buy the tickets on Monday."

"So, shall we meet at Leicester Square? Let's say half an hour before it begins. Does that sound correct?"

"I thought you might come to Twickenham in the afternoon. I could pick you up at the railway station and have a drink with you in my flat before going to Central London."

"All right but... We don't know each other yet."

"It would be a nice way to get to know each other."

"The problem is that I have promised to see my sister's daughter in the afternoon, for her birthday. I'm sorry, but I think I can't miss It."

"I understand, of course. We'll meet at Leicester Square then. Call me on Monday evening so that I can tell you what time the musical starts."

"No problem... I'm looking forward to seeing you. I really like your voice, you know."

John was extremely surprised and happy.

"Thank you," he answered, "we'll talk on Monday."

"Bye bye then."

"Bye, Emily."

The next day, he picked up his daughter at his former wife's flat and took her to Twickenham. They had lunch together before doing some shopping. By the end of the afternoon, he helped her with some homework. He only had a look at his email box in the evening. He had received several messages from women he had never chatted with. He was planning to surf on the internet when Sarah asked him to watch a DVD film with her. He realized then that connecting to a dating site every night wasn't a sensible attitude. Spending time with his daughter was more important, and he already had a date with Emily, so he contented himself with answering the messages politely and turned his computer off.

On Sunday, he took Sarah to the Design Museum in the morning; she had a lot of fun there. They had a picnic next to the Globe Theatre before going to the Tate Modern where they spent about an hour.

"I love those paintings", she said as they were leaving the Gallery.

"You like modern art, don't you?"

"Especially Mark Rothko. I'm keen on his colours. What about you, Dad?"

"I prefer painters like Dali and Picasso."

"Oh, I like them too."

"Very good for a ten-year-old little girl; you already know a lot about painting, don't you?"

"Shall we cross over to the other side of the Millennium Bridge?"

"Why not?"

"Do you know I've never been across it?"

"Really?"

"That's true, Dad."

"Let's go then. Once on the north bank, we'll take a bus to Covent Garden. We'll see if there's any interesting attraction there."

"All right. Shall we go to the London Transport Museum if there isn't any? A friend of mine said he had enjoyed it."

At Covent Garden, they watched a juggler for a while, then it was time for Sarah to go home.

"I"ll take you to the museum next time."

"O.K. We mustn't keep Mum waiting."

The weekend was soon over. He went back to work; on Monday evening, Emily called him. He had bought tickets for the 8 o'clock performance, so he suggested that they met at quarter past seven on Saturday. He had news from Harry on Wednesday evening.

"Hello, Harry. How did it go with the lovely blonde from Brighton?

"It was a mess."

"What do you mean, a mess?"

"A real mess, John."

"What happened?"

"Sonia made me mad. She's a prostitute, you know!"

"A prostitute!"

"Yes, on the site she claimed to be an ordinary young woman seeking fun, nothing more. She really got me in."

"How did you learn who she was?"

"She asked me for money as soon as we arrived here. We had been in the living-room for a quarter of an hour or so, she was in my arms, a real beauty, you know. All that was too easy. Then she said 'all right, if you want some more, give me 200 pounds; 500 and I'll stay overnight'.

"How amazed you must have been!"

"Of course I was. I refused, but she said it was unfair, I couldn't allow myself to make her waste her time. So I tried to throw her out. Do you know what she did?"

"Difficult to imagine. I suppose she didn't leave your flat quietly."

"Sure she didn't. She started screaming like a sow. 'Harry Portman is a fucking wanker! Harry Portman is a fucking bastard! Harry Portman is a silly bugger! Harry Portman is... And so on. The neighbours must have heard. There was no way to make her stop shouting."

"How did that story end up?"

"I got rid of her with two fifty-pound notes. 'I can undress for you for 100', she said, and she started to take her clothes off. I just said 'no, go away now', which she did, adding that I just had to fuck off!"

"Charming! My poor Harry, what a dreadful time you must have had. I was thinking of you on Saturday evening, as Sarah and I were watching a film. In my mind, you were supposed to be having such a great time!"

"I was actually getting high on an enormous pizza and a bottle of wine to forget Sonia, which is certainly not her real name, and that bloody site."

"Don't be so bitter. It must have happened before to unfortunate guys like you. That'll be O.K. next time. As for me, I hope I'll be luckier with Emily."

"Who's Emily?"

"The one I am to meet on Saturday evening. We're going to watch a musical, 'Chicago'. She's quite learned, she sounds very nice. She must be cute."

"Don't you think you should have a drink with her before going to the theatre together, just to know what she looks like?"

"That won't be necessary. I'm quite optimistic about her physical appearance. I can't be mistaken. Anyway, she doesn't know what I look like either."

"How will you recognize each other then?"

"She'll be wearing a long black coat and a red scarf. As for me, I'll have my brown leather jacket and a beige tie on. I think we can't miss each other."

"All that sounds so romantic! Have a lot of fun, and give me some news."

"I won't forget. I'll call you soon. Bye."

John didn't chat with anybody on the internet for the rest of the week. He only answered this message he received on Friday :

"Dear John,

I've been ever so happy since I first spoke to you. I still can hear your charming voice, just as if you were speaking to me now. I'm looking forward to being with you at the theatre and I really hope we'll have a great time together.

Best regards,

Emily"

He was enthralled by such thoughtfulness. For a few minutes he hesitated, then he started writing:

"Dear Emily,

Thank you so much for sending me such a kind message. I will be delighted to spend the whole Saturday evening in your company. Please don't forget to wear your red scarf. I'm sure we will both enjoy the musical.

Friendly,
John"

In spite of his belief that he would by no means be disappointed, he couldn't help thinking of what had happened to Harry. What if he thought too well of Emily? In fact, he was just feeling anxious, like a young man before his first date.

On Saturday, he took the train to Waterloo Station by quarter past six, then the Northern Line to Leicester Square. The underground was crowded with people walking in and out; some were going back home after spending the afternoon in shops, cinemas or public gardens while others were about to enjoy themselves in restaurants, pubs, theatres, night clubs and discotheques. He came out of the station at twenty to eight and found himself standing in the middle of the square one minute later. He had always loved the place. When he came there with Sarah, they always went to Haagen Dazs ice-cream parlour for her to taste new flavours. 'I can see no one with a long black coat and a red scarf on,' he concluded after looking around him, 'except this fat woman standing next to the statue of William Shakespeare, who's smiling at me, but she can't be Emily'. He retraced his steps to the north side entrance. There was a long queue in front of The Empire. He turned back and looked again. The statue of the world-famous bard caught his eye. He walked towards it; the huge woman hadn't moved. He stopped in front of it and read the motto: 'There is no darkness but ignorance.'

"What do you think of this?" she asked.

"What?"

"I was just asking you..."

"... Oh, the motto! The darkness I'm expecting is a long black coat, and I think the lady supposed to wear it won't be long."

"Is she also supposed to wear a red scarf?"

"She actually is!"

"So you are John, aren't you?"

He suddenly became aware that he was facing Emily, the woman in a long dark coat he had ignored a few minutes before.

"Are you...?"

He didn't finish his sentence. How could she be?

"I am! What a pleasure to see you at last! Shall we go to Cambridge Theatre now? It's in Earlham Street, is it what you told me?"

"Er... Yes, indeed. Er... Let's go then."

They headed for the theatre, walking side by side. She looked radiant with happiness whereas he was upset. He didn't have the heart to say that he was no longer feeling like going to the musical with her. 'She's so fat! Five feet seven inches, all right, nine stones six pounds, bollocks! What about the four stones she forgot to mention? To hell with that bloody liar!' As he didn't consider himself as a boor, he decided that he would just be polite; he would behave like a gentleman. He would say goodbye after the performance and the whole story would be over.

He didn't talk much on the way. She felt his disappointment as well as she obviously knew the reason for it.

"If I had told you the truth, you wouldn't have invited me, would you? You wouldn't even have answered my first message!" she said as they were entering Cambridge Theatre.

"Let's find our seats, shall we?" he said as if he hadn't heard, "Here they are. Make yourself comfortable."

"I know you're angry with me and I understand that you're feeling so. Thank you for being kind."

"I'm just trying to make things as pleasant as they can be. I hope you'll have a nice time watching the show", he answered, though thinking 'Shut up, don't make things worse. Just watch and leave me alone.'

The first part was followed by a fifteen-minute interval during which they compared their impressions. They were both enthusiastic.

"John! John Drummond!" he heard all of a sudden. He turned round and recognized Robert Bradford. 'My worst enemy,' he thought, 'on Monday morning, everybody in the business will know about Emily and me. Oh, my god!'

"Hello, Robert."

"You remember Gloria, don't you?"

"Of course," he answered, standing up, "hello, Gloria."

He hoped that they wouldn't realize that he wasn't alone. Robert was the boss of a rival estate agency in Twickenham; he hated John. His wife was young, splendid and full of charm.

"Did you come here on your own?" Robert asked mischievously. He had just noticed Emily who, at the same moment, made a sign to him. "Why don't you introduce your girlfriend?" he remarked, speaking up for everyone around to hear him.

"In fact, Emily is..."

"Hello, Emily! Nice to meet you. This is Gloria, my dear wife!"

"Hello, Gloria. Hello, Robert. I'm so glad to meet John's friends."

"Well, Emily loves musicals, so..."

"There's nothing to explain! You're full of mysteries, you lucky devil ! Isn't he, Gloria?"

Gloria stretched her long body to make herself taller and even slimmer.

The lights faded. The time had come for the spectators to go back to their seats. John was relieved. Yet he watched the second part quite absent-mindedly. He should at all costs avoid finding himself face to face with Robert and Gloria again when they left the theatre, which he eventually managed to do.

Emily and he were heading for the underground station when she broke the silence.

"John, you asked me the other day if I would agree about having a drink with you, do you remember?"

He didn't answer.

"You wanted me to go to your flat before coming here. I mean, I wouldn't mind now if we..."

"... I will take you home, then we'll say goodbye", he replied.

"What about having a drink in my own place, then?"

"I don't think it would be a good idea. Anyway, I will just have enough time to go back to Waterloo Station and catch the last train."

They took the underground at Covent Garden. When they arrived in front of her door, Emily renewed her invitation. Once again, John refused.

"You wouldn't say 'no' if I looked like Gloria."

"I don't think I would agree. I don't like her."

"You don't like me either."

"I certainly like you better than I like her, but that's not the point."

"What's the point, then? You don't dislike me but I'm too fat, so I don't deserve your attention."

"Not as a lover. I'm sorry."

"Did I ask you to make love with me?"

"You didn't, but you know as well as I do it's a lover you're looking for. Otherwise you wouldn't have registered on that site. As far as I remember, you didn't mention that you were only seeking friendship, but love relationship, which indeed doesn't mean that you're ready to spend the night with a man you hardly know! But as long as you lie about your physical appearance, you will be disappointed. I just hope you will find the man you deserve, but you'll have to find a better way for that."

Emily started to cry.

"I didn't mean to hurt you."

"I know you didn't. I'm just ashamed of myself."

"Forget about it. The musical was good, anyway."

"Yes, but... The thing is, if you had proposed to spend the night with me, I would have accepted. A woman like me has no alternative; I was born fat, I've grown fat and I'll always be bloody fat, even if I go on a hundred fucking diets!"

"I'm really sorry. If there's anything..."

"... You've been kind to me, I appreciate. You're a very nice man, John. I don't want to make you late, you'd better go now."

"Good night then; good luck!"

"Thank you. Good night."

When at last he could sit on his sofa, he was still thinking of her distress. 'What an ugly world', he reflected, 'life isn't fair sometimes. I'm sure Emily is a good girl, but she's desperate for happiness and I'm afraid she'll always be'.

He didn't feel sleepy at all, so he switched his computer on and sent a message to the dating site webmaster for his registration to be cancelled.

"Farewell, Jdrum! Goodbye, the lean, the fat, the plump, the small and the tall ones, the bloody liars, the frustrated, the perverse and the sex maniacs, the exhibitionists and the viewers! Goodbye Monica 3616, Ginger 7153, Emma 2977, Adriana 4663! Goodbye you all. John Drummond is going back to real life!"

May half-term holidays began the weekend after. John was to spend four days in France with Sarah and was eager to go there. As he had bought tickets for the 9.25 ferry to Calais, they left London early on Sunday morning. The road to Dover wasn't busy; they had cleared the English customs by quarter to nine. Sarah had already been to France with her parents in the past but it was the first time she had been there alone with her father. They were going to the Côtes d'Armor, in Brittany. John had friends there, a couple with two children, a twelve-year-old son and a daughter who was the same age as Sarah. He was happy to see them again.

"Paulo, je suis si content; ça fait neuf ans, n'est-ce pas?"

"Neuf ans déjà ! Le temps passe si vite!"

"Bonjour, Françoise. Voici Sarah."

The little girl wasn't surprised to see her father shake hands with their host and kiss their hostess, a French custom she was used to.

"Sarah, here are Françoise and Jean-Paul."

"Bonjour," she said, "are Yohann and Gaëlle here?"

"Ils ne vont pas tarder... Euh..."

"All right", Sarah nodded.

"Tu as compris? They are... Paulo, comment on dit, déjà?"

"Horse-riding. Ah, les voilà, justement."

Françoise and Jean-Paul, like the majority of French people, were far from being keen on foreign languages, and their ignorance of English, which they had learnt at school for seven years, had no equal but their deplorable accent.

Sarah spent a nice evening playing with Gaëlle while Yohann was busy with some video game. In the meantime, John and Jean-Paul were making plans for the next day.

"Will you come with me in the morning? I'll show you my new office."

Jean-Paul was an architect at Saint-Quay Portrieux.

"I'll be happy, of course. I suppose Sarah will get some sleep, so I'll be back here by, let's say... half past ten. I'll take her to the beach in the afternoon if the weather is still fine. Françoise may come with us, as she leaves work by midday."

"Sure", she answered.

"All right, and I'll take you to the restaurant in the evening."

"Thank you, John. That's very nice", Jean-Paul agreed. "I think the children will have dinner together at home."

Things were settled. There is no half-term holiday in France as the school year is over by the beginning of July. So John had to organize himself for his daughter not to feel lonely during the day while her new friends were at school. On Monday, the weather was exceptionally warm, which allowed them to spend two hours on the beach in the afternoon with Françoise. On Tuesday morning the rain was back and the temperature had dropped a great deal. 'Le crachin breton', as Jean-Paul said, 'it won't last. We might even have a sunny afternoon!' Breton optimism! John and Sarah spent most of the day inside, hoping the rain would stop. It did for a while, so they seized the opportunity of this bright interval to walk to the centre of Saint-Quay. Sarah bought some souvenir for her mother and John purchased a leather shoulder bag. On the way back, they met Françoise and Jean-Paul's female neighbour.

"Bonjour", they said.

"Bonjour. Nice to hear people speak English in the neighbourhood!"

"Nice to hear somebody speak good English here!" John replied.

"I actually spend most of my time in London. I work there!"

"Do you? I live and work in Twickenham."

"Really? I work in Hounslow. That's not very far."

She was really attractive, about his age, maybe a little younger. He learnt from his friends that she was single, and thought it was a real pity he didn't have time to get to know her better. He drove back to Calais on Wednesday and dropped Sarah off in front of her mother's house in the evening. He went back to work the next day, after this short but enjoyable and salutary break. He had forgotten about the dating site, about Emily, but he felt alone once back home. Although he was professionally successful, his private life was a failure.

He was understandably happy, under such circumstances, to meet his new next door neighbour who, as he was to learn later, was a recently divorced thirty-two-year old childless brunette who had just moved in. She, as a matter of fact, knocked at his door on Friday evening to ask him for help.

"I'm sorry to disturb you, but my computer seems to have broken down. I can't switch it on any more. Would you be so kind as to help me?"

"All right. I'm not a specialist, you know, but I'll see if I can do something for you."

"That's fine. Thank you ever so much."

"Don't mention it."

He followed her into her flat. He felt quite fortunate about her being so charming.

"My name's Vicki."

"I'm glad to know you, Vicki. Please call me John!"

She showed him into her small office.

"Here it is!"

"Let me see. It doesn't seem to work, actually. Is it plugged in properly?"

"I think so."

John took off the plug and inserted it into the wall socket again, then he switched the computer on without difficulty.

"That's it. Everything's all right now."

"Oh, thank you for your help."

"That's nothing, Vicki."

She offered him a drink in the living-room. She was rather talkative; a lively woman with a curious mind who painted watercolours she hung on the walls of each room. They chatted nicely for half an hour until he left.

"Have a nice evening working on your computer."

"Good evening. See you, John."

"See you, Vicki."

On Saturday afternoon, after speaking to Sarah on the phone, he felt like seeing Vicki again. He had been thinking of her all morning. What about asking her for a walk? They actually hardly knew each other and he didn't want to appear intrusive. It would prove very easy yet to knock at her door and suggest going out. After hesitating for a while, he decided that was the best thing to do. Unfortunately she seemed to be busy doing something else since he got no answer. He felt a little disappointed but the weekend was far from being over, so he would chance his luck again on the morrow.

Harry called him on Sunday morning. He sounded enthusiastic.

"I've been lucky this time, John", he said.

"What are you talking about? Business? Women?"

"Women, John! Women! Well, I mean, the woman I met yesterday is gorgeous!"

"Did you meet her on the internet?"

"I did, actually. You see, you may be disappointed with those dating sites, but when it works, it's wonderful. You talk to people you'd have crossed in the street without ever speaking to them."

"I think it's much more pleasant to make somebody's acquaintance in the real life."

"Don't be so defeatist! Your experience with Emily has been very unfortunate, but I know you're not a loser, John. Try again!"

"Certainly not. I'm perfectly aware now that I'm not keen on dating sites. I will never try again."

"All right. It's up to you."

"What is she like?"

"Quite pretty, very nice, easy-going. We met yesterday; we spent the afternoon together in Kew Gardens, then we had dinner in town and she went back home."

"How romantic!"

She isn't the kind of woman who looks for sex, you know. What she wants is a lasting relation with a man she can trust."

"Very good. You think you're the one she can trust, don't you?"

"Don't you think I am a reliable man?"

"I see. You've fallen in love with her, haven't you?"

"She really is the kind of girl one doesn't meet every day, you know."

"So, when are you seeing her again?"

"During the week, and next weekend."

"O.K. Don't forget to invite me to your wedding."

"I promise. You'll be the best man!"

They both laughed about it, though thinking that might happen. Harry was thirty-five and had never been married; John, although he had been joking, was persuaded he was ready for that. He had never shown any eagerness to meet a woman who might become his wife so far. He had had a few girlfriends; some had even been known to go out with him quite long, but this time it was different. What mostly surprised John was the fact that he had just told him about a woman who wasn't his girlfriend yet as if he were already planning to marry her. 'Wait and see', he thought, 'Harry seems to be a happy man. He has met a nice lady. So have I!"

He got up from the sofa and went next door at once to ask his lovely neighbour if, by chance, she was free for an afternoon walk. She actually was, and joyfully accepted his invitation. Unfortunately it started raining by two o'clock, as they were about to leave John's flat.

"Let's stay here, then", he suggested. "What about a cup of tea?"

"I'd rather have a glass of white wine. I have some in my fridge, it's cool and nice."

"Very good idea indeed. I love white wine!"

"I'll go and get it then. I won't be a minute."

Vicki came back with a bottle and a book.

"You told me on Friday you like watercolours. I've brought this. Have you heard of Marie Laurencin?"

"Maybe. I'm not certain."

"She was a French artist in the first half of the twentieth century. She was a self-taught painter, remembered as a feminine cubist and Guillaume Apollinaire's muse, as well as a Parisian femme fatale."

"I've never seen any of her paintings, but I think I've heard her name before. Wasn't it... Let me think... Oh yes, I remember now ; a song by Joe Dassin, a French singer who was successful in the seventies. 'Avec ta robe longue, tu ressemblais à une aquarelle de Marie Laurencin', from 'L'Été Indien'. Have you heard it? »

"No. What does it mean? It's about a dress, isn't it?"

"It means 'In your long dress, you looked like a watercolour by Marie Laurencin'. Shall we have a look?"

They went through the book while drinking. They had almost finished the bottle of wine by the time she closed it.

"Another glass?" John suggested.

"Yes, please. There won't be enough for you, I'm

afraid."

"Never mind. Just finish it and I'll get some champagne."

"Are you sure?"

"Don't you like champagne?"

"Of course I do."

"Good."

They went on chatting, joking and laughing until they got half-drunk, and finally made love on the sofa.

The days that followed, they had no opportunity to see each other. John came back from work very late on Monday and Tuesday evenings and did not dare to bother Vicki. On Wednesday, as he was at home by eight, he knocked at her door but he got no answer. He was quite amazed; she hadn't tried to get in touch with him since Sunday. It was as if she avoided him, but he didn't understand why. He had the opportunity to speak to her at last on Thursday morning as they were both leaving for work.

"Vicki, I'm glad to see you. I..."

"Hi John, I'm sorry, I'm in a hurry."

"Well, can't we speak...?"

"I'm late, you know. Could we have a talk tomorrow night?"

"Why not tonight?"

"I will be busy."

"Tomorrow then."

"O.K. for tomorrow."

"Let's have dinner together!"

"Well..."

"Dinner at home, all right?"

"O.K. for dinner."

"See you tomorrow night!"

"See you , John."

She was strange. She no longer was the enthusiastic young woman he had made love with on Sunday. Did she regret? Was she ashamed? Was she afraid of being judged by a man she had given herself to whereas she had just met him? She had accepted to have dinner with him anyway. Maybe she had to deal with some personal matter which had nothing to do with their relationship.

He was a little tense on Friday evening. When she entered his flat, he could easily guess that she was ill-at-ease, which didn't make the situation easy for him either. They talked about their professional activities until the moment when John suggested that they had some dessert.

"No, thanks", Vicki answered.

"I won't have any either."

"You can, if you want to."

"No, I just would like to talk about..."

"... About...?"

"...Sunday afternoon. I mean..."

"That's what I would like to talk about as well."

"Fine. I understand it may not be easy."

"It isn't indeed. You know... I don't want you to be shocked but..."

"... You've done nothing shocking. Maybe all that happened earlier than we expected, but you don't have to feel uneasy about it."

"I do feel uneasy about it, John, and I don't want it to happen again."

"Do you mean...?"

"I don't mean to hurt you."

"Do you regret?"

"There's no point in having regrets. We had a good time making love, but it was a mistake."

"I see. I thought that... I must have been stupid to believe we had been starting something."

"I'm really sorry, John. You're a nice man, you know."

"I'm afraid I've heard that before. A fat lot of good that does me!"

"The truth is... Last Friday, I needed my computer to chat with a man."

"Do you mean you've registered on a dating site?"

"I do, and I saw this man for the first time on Saturday afternoon. I was with him yesterday evening. I do think he's in love with me and..."

"... And you do think you're in love with him!"

"That's true. The strange thing is that nothing has happened between us so far. You know what I mean."

"I think I do. You make love with a man you don't love because what he may think about you doesn't matter, but when you're in love, you..."

"I'm ashamed, John! Believe me. I had never behaved like that before. It's the first time things have been going on this way. I understand why you're so angry with me. If you think I deserve your anger, then you're right to blame me."

"Well, I didn't mean to blame you. I must be honest and blame myself as well. I don't think you deserve my anger. We'd better forget about all this. We had a nice time; let's not spoil it."

"I agree with you. Thank you for understanding me. You really are a good man, and I am certain that you will meet the woman you deserve... I think I should go home now. Good night."

"Good night, Vicki."

Although John 'understood', he had a rough time that weekend. Fortunately Sarah helped him forget a little about that sad adventure which he found a bitter pill to swallow. His colleagues at work asked him several times along the week if he was all right. He felt bad and didn't manage to conceal it.

On Wednesday he had lunch in a pub with Harry.

"What's the hell, John?"

"There's no hell, Harry."

"You look rotten, I can tell you."

"Everybody bothers me about that; they all ask me what I feel like. I'm just overworked."

"All right. Let's say you're overworked."

"You'd better tell me about you and ..."

"Vicki!"

"Vicki?"

"Vicki! What's the matter?"

"Nothing. Just go on."

"Oh, I didn't tell you. She lives in Twickenham."

"She might live in my street. Who knows?"

John was suddenly sure that his female neighbour had fallen in love with his friend Harry. 'Bloody internet', he thought, 'the hell with sex on the internet.' But this time, a kind of miracle had happened. It wasn't a matter of sex, but a matter of love! 'Sex with me, love with Harry! Why not the opposite? Why not just L.O.V.E. with me?'

"I don't know her address."

"A discreet woman! Not the kind who logs in to have fun with a different man every weekend!"

"Not at all. I told you, John. We've just kissed each other. Nothing else."

'My god. He's going to tell me about his love affair as if we were still at secondary school! I know the whole story, mate! Will you take the plunge this weekend? All right, I can tell you making love with her is fine. How childish!'

"John, what are you thinking about?"

"Vicki."

"Vicki?"

"Vicki! How lucky you are!"

"I know I am. I hope I'll introduce her to you soon."

"I'm looking forward to it. The best man's privilege, isn't it?"

Week after week, John became more and more pessimistic about his own fate. He had lost confidence, persuaded as he was that no woman would ever get any real interest in him. His only care for his private life was Sarah whom he got on with better and better; a marvellous aspect of his existence which nonetheless couldn't make up for the sentimental void.

As for Harry, he never had the opportunity to introduce Vicki to John until a fortnight before the wedding. They avoided to be brought face to face. When Vicki seemed to agree about a possible meeting, John wasn't free. When he agreed, she had something else to do.

Harry found it rather unfortunate and felt sorry, but he didn't suspect that they did everything they could to make it unfeasible; it didn't come to his mind either that they might have some particular reason for doing so. Indeed he had come to know that they were neighbours, a fact that hadn't been concealed from him very long. Yet the best man and the bride-to-be couldn't but be officially introduced by the bridegroom himself before the great day. All he knew from his future wife was that they had had some rare opportunities to see each other and talk. He finally managed to invite John to his place for a meal, so that the three of them could spend a couple of hours together. No sign of intimacy between Vicki and John could be perceived as evident.

John hadn't forgotten what had been going on one Sunday afternoon. He still felt depressed; moreover he wasn't very enthusiastic about going to the wedding which was to take place a few days before Christmas in the north of London, in a large estate which was said to have been owned by somebody famous, probably a British film director who had recently died. He had found it for Harry who called him the day before the event to express his great satisfaction and his gratitude.

"Everything's ready. It will be great thanks to you. This place is really wonderful. For Vicki, it's like a dream."

"I'm happy you both like it."

He certainly was, but he wasn't ready to smile at people he didn't know, make a speech for his friend in front of all of them and congratulate a bride he had slept with. Nevertheless he knew he had to be there because he couldn't deceive Harry, and Sarah, who would be among the guests, was looking forward to being introduced to the audience as the best man's daughter.

"We are ever so grateful to you, John. Vicki insists that I thank you again. By the way, you've got friends somewhere in Brittany, haven't you? Is that saint-Quay..."

"... Portrieux."

"Saint-Quay Portrieux, all right. Vicki has a close friend who's got a house there, a Frenchwoman about our age, I mean, let's say around thirty-five, who works in London, and she thought she might be your dancing partner."

"A Frenchwoman who works in London! I hope she's nice."

"According to Vicki, she really is, and she's very attractive."

"Fine. I will be happy to know her."

After hanging up, he thought of Françoise and Jean-Paul's neighbour whom he had briefly met at the beginning of May, but he immediately forgot this idea for fear of being once more disappointed.

When he arrived at the city hall, the next day, he was introduced to the bride and groom-to-be's relatives and friends. After greeting them all, he hardly remembered more than three or four names, which unquestionably wasn't a cause for concern, contrary to the fact that he hadn't met the woman he was to spend the whole day with; even if he didn't want to believe in such a coincidence, he secretly hoped that she was the one he expected. Suddenly, Harry gave him a dig in the ribs.

"What's going on?" he asked.

"Look at her. She must be Marianne. I've never met her before, but I'm sure she is."

"She actually is!" John answered, smiling.

"How do you know?"

"She's my French friends' neighbour!"

"... Is she? How incredible!"

"Hello, John, what a surprise!" Marianne exclaimed, "I didn't expect... Well, I'm so happy!"

"You can't be happier than I am!"

Marianne wasn't only pretty; she was also merry, witty and kind, which confirmed John's first impression. A day which he would remember as happily memorable had just begun.

TWIST OF FATE

Alan, with Lea on his arm, was looking at Saint Sauveur Cathedral tower. Bruges, the Belgian Venice, was majestic and quiet under the sun of February. The loud sound of horseshoes pounding the paving stones regularly disturbed the silence. When the passengers got off the carriages, often with great regret, they headed for some chocolate shop. Alan and Lea had decided to wait until the day before their departure to buy four or five pounds of dark, milk and hazelnut chocolate they would offer. They would do the same with some of the three hundred and fifty or more brands of beer which can be found in Belgium.

They walked until they found the Groeninge Museum. Alan spotted a tobacco shop not far from the entrance.

"I'll buy some cigarettes. What about you?"

"I'll buy a carton. They are less than half price compared with England."

"You're right. I think I'll have a carton as well."

After buying their cigarettes, they smoked on the pavement before entering the museum. They were both fascinated by the first exhibition room; Alan was particularly attracted by 'the Judgment of Cambyses', which frightened Lea who preferred 'the Garden of Earthly Delights'.

"It's horrible to see this poor man being flayed alive. It scared me as soon as we entered the room!"

Alan explained to Lea that the judge represented

in Gerard David's diptych was corrupt and had been sentenced to death by the tribunal.

"His son", he added, "who was to be in office after his father, had to watch the executioners put him to death."

"How barbaric!"

"They did it for him not to be tempted by corruption and be a better and more honest judge than his father had been."

"Hieronymus Bosch's painting is much more pleasant to watch, anyway. I like it. All those characters in the central panel look funny, don't they?"

"They actually do. If one day you have the opportunity to go to the Prado, you'll see the original which is bigger than this copy."

"Why 'you'? You mean 'if one day we have the opportunity', don't you? I would like to go to Madrid with you!"

She frowned.

"I don't mean you have to go to Spain on your own. I... Never mind, forget it, let's go on!"

She stopped frowning.

When the visit was over, they went to the Memling Museum. Later, they had dinner in a small restaurant. The next morning, Alan went to a car rental company from which he had hired a Small Peugeot.

He was smoking a Virginia cigarette on the way. It was a little chilly; the weather forecast had said it would be sunny all day long but a little cold for the season. The distance between Bruges and Ghent was only twenty-five miles; the trip would be short. He was eager to visit the Design Museum. Lea was in principle more interested in the Museum of Contemporary Art. She was pretty and young, a little plump, and childish, a kind of 'femme-enfant' he had been attracted by two years before, who was getting on his nerves now as she showed a more and more obvious tendency to see him as a father.

He was back to the hotel by nine. They had time to walk round Ghent before lunch. At the beginning of the afternoon, Alan was greatly disappointed with contemporary art. Five minutes after going into the museum, he was already out. He had a drink in the cafeteria until Lea was back, rather satisfied, an hour later.

"Did you enjoy it?" she asked, half-convinced.

"I only stayed five minutes."

"Why? Not everything is good, but altogether, I found it quite enjoyable."

"Good for you if you liked it. Personally I don't think that three branches lain on the floor are meant to be a work of art. Such guys won't fool me into making me believe they are artists!"

"Why can't it be a work of art? Isn't nature a work of art?"

"If nature is a work of art, they should leave it alone then! What about those ten big books with blank pages in a cold white one-hundred-and-fifty-square-yard room? What on earth is the meaning of that?"

"It's the symbol of nothingness, isn't it?"

"I would say that, as far as books represent the basis of knowledge, the blankness of the pages is the expression of human ignorance! So what?"

"So this is contemporary art!"

"So this is no more than shitting on an exhibition table and claiming the transformation of the crap day after day is the symbol of human degeneration! The only kind of art I see in it is short-lived art, and I think it's a paradox!"

"Why can't art be ephemeral?"

"Because it is part of culture, civilisation; it is part of human memory. It is a precious link between our past and our present."

"I don't see things this way, but you must be much more intelligent than me!"

"Never mind. I would like to take you to a funny place, the 'one-thousand-and-one-night' sauna. It's mixed. A friend of mine has heartily recommended it to me."

"Mixed?"

"Yes. What's the trouble ?"

"The trouble simply is that it's mixed!"

"Don't worry about that!"

"But everybody will be..."

"Naked? What do you think? Do you imagine you will go to such a place in one of your evening dresses?"

"But... Why don't people wear bathing costumes, for instance?"

"Oh, stop pussyfooting around and come with me."

He took her by the hand to drag her off to the sauna house where they met a smiling receptionist who handed them two bathrobes. Lea was reluctant to take it.

"I'm not sure I want to go in", she said.

"Come on, Lea. Take this bathrobe!"

"I understand you may feel embarrassed," the woman went on.

"I surely do, but he doesn't understand."

"Everybody does, I mean the first time, but they quickly get used to being naked. After five minutes, you'll have forgotten your apprehension and you won't pay attention any more."

"That's sounds sensible. You aren't a little girl. Let's go."

Despite what he had just said, Lea was, in some sort of way, a 'little girl' in Alan's mind, even though he wouldn't admit it as true. He was sixty years old, had been married twice; she was twenty-five. One day, in a clothes shop in London, the assistant had told him that 'his daughter' really looked beautiful in the flounced dress she had just been trying on. He had been so horribly vexed that he had left for home at once, leaving Lea behind. This was yet the sort of inconvenience he had exposed himself to as soon as he had started a love relationship with a woman who was about thirty-five years younger than him, and who, moreover, was younger than Tom, his twenty-nine-year-old son and Tina, his twenty-six-year-old 'legitimate' daughter, both from his first marriage which had lasted almost two decades. Although he sometimes reproached her for being immature, he didn't hesitate to treat her as a child who was supposed to obey him, which obviously made their everyday life less and less easy.

She followed him silently into the cloakroom where she undressed quickly and wrapped herself in the bathrobe. The room they entered next was dimly lit. The dark red lights only allowed to have a glimpse of the silhouettes and kept the bodies partly hidden. After hesitating for a few seconds, she took her bathrobe off and had a shower next to unknown people. Inside the sauna, it was very hot and she found it nice. It proved more difficult for Alan to deal with the heat.

"I think it's time to get out of here", he proposed after only a few minutes.

"Not yet. I'm enjoying it. I'm staying."

"Do you mean you're going to remain here alone, naked?"

"I'm sorry, I've forgotten to bring my evening dress! Look, Alan, you've insisted on bringing me to this place, you've blamed me for being childish because I didn't want to show my bottom and my breasts, and now you're about to make a fuss because I intend to stay here alone, lying on this bench just because I'm topless and I've got my fanny bare? Are you crazy?"

As he was about to answer, a couple entered. The man was quite tall and lean; the woman was taller and overweight. Alan sat silent for a while, then he stood up and told her that he wanted to go into the hammam. Lea rose slowly and stretched her body nonchalantly, her back turned on the man who was lying on a wooden bench next to his fat wife. She went out of the sauna, self-satisfied and triumphant. She knew he was looking at her buttocks.

Contrary to the sauna which was brightly lit, the hammam was dark, full of steam. She sat and snuggled up to Alan for almost half an hour before going upstairs. The room there was furnished with a dozen canopy beds on which people could lie, drink as much fruit juice as they wanted and eat sweets, peanuts, raisins, cashew nuts and clementines. Several couples were already relaxing. Alan and Lea chose a bed and talked happily, forgetting their argument in the sauna, until they fell asleep, curled up in their bathrobes, facing each other.

Their day in Ghent ended in a pub. In the morning, it was Lea who took the Peugeot back to the car rental company. She gave Alan a kiss before leaving.

When she came back, he wasn't in the hotel room.

"Alan, are you in the bathroom?"

She got no answer. She checked and realized he wasn't there. She thought he might have gone to the reception for some reason, or to the newsagent's across the street to buy 'The Guardian', as he sometimes did at home.

She looked through the window; she could see the belfry overhanging the peaceful town. She loved London indeed, but it was so noisy, so huge. Bruges made her feel good. She turned back and stepped away from the window. Suddenly, she caught sight of an envelope on the table. Her name was written on it. In a fit of fear, she opened the cupboard and found out his clothes and his suitcase had disappeared. With beating heart, she read the letter.

Dear Lea,

We've been together for two years now, and I must say we've had wonderful moments, but the summer of your life is only at a start whereas the autumn of mine will soon come to an end. Despite the fact that we love each other, this very difference also implies that we're living in worlds apart. We've been arguing lately, as we did yesterday. It's so stupid, I know, but the gap between us has made it ineluctable.

I'm sorry, but I can no longer stay here with you. I'm going back to London. I've paid the hotel bill, and you will find your train ticket in the table drawer.

I love you, but I must go.

Alan

P.S. Please don't come to my place when you're back home. It will be fine if you stay in your flat.

She felt as if she had been turned into stone; her legs and her arms were too heavy to move, her body seemed to be disconnected from her mind.

"How can you allow yourself to leave me on my own? What have I done wrong? You could have spoken to me instead of... Fucking hell, you're older than me, I don't care. I love you, fucking idiot! I hate you for what you've done, and I know as well I'm silly enough to forgive you because I'm foolish, because I'm a good girl, because I fucking love you, bloody twit! What shall I do now, alone, like a poor damn thing?" she uttered aloud, in tears.

She flopped down onto the bed and remained motionless.

Alan had just got into the 9.30 train. It was twenty past nine. He was thinking of Lea who had certainly been reading his letter. He was wondering whether she was furious, disappointed, dubious or devastated. On the platform, he had expected her to turn up, breathless, dishevelled, desperately looking for him. She hadn't, but he still hoped she would show up at the very last moment, like in a film, to prevent him from leaving. In the first version, romantic enough, he would have time to get off, he would take her in his arms and give her a long kiss; in the second one, the very romantic one, the dramatic one also, it would be too late; he would get up and hurry towards the door to open it, but the train would be on motion and she would run on the platform to prolong the instant, the tragic moment when she understood he would never come back and she would never see him again... Whatever might happen, they both lived in London and would see each other again if they wanted to, so there was indeed but little drama and romance in the reality of their existence.

Alan had been back to London for five days; he had no news from Lea. He didn't know if she had stayed in Bruges or not after he had left. Even if she had, she was supposed to be back anyway. He missed her, but he thought that calling her would be disrespectful for he was the one who had left without notice.

Tom and his wife, Hanna, a tall blonde from the Czech Republic, came to see him on the weekend. They had a one-year-old son named Robin. Alan was always happy to spend some time with Tom, but he wasn't interested in his grandson who was noisy and fidgety; as for his daughter-in-law, he thought she had no personality and very little charm. She was just kind and smiling. They arrived in Richmond on Saturday morning and left on Sunday afternoon. Their presence allowed him not to think of Lea all the time. When Hanna alluded to their holiday in Bruges, he answered evasively and changed the subject.

He unsuccessfully tried to call his girlfriend as soon as they had left. On Monday morning, he called her again by the time she was used to getting up on working days. Later he phoned her company, but there was no way for him to be put through with her office. He thought something was going wrong, so he decided to wait for her outside the firm building by five o'clock. He didn't see her come out but he saw Bridget, a colleague of hers he had met several times. He went and met her to try and get some information.

"Hello, Bridget. Do you remember me? I'm Alan."

"Of course", she answered, visibly embarrassed.

"Have you seen Lea?"

"I'm sorry, I haven't seen her."

"Was she in today?"

"I'm afraid she wasn't."

"Do you know why she was absent?"

"I... I don't."

"Nobody wants to tell me anything about Lea! That's so strange!"

"I have nothing to tell you."

"You're her friend, aren't you? So, please!"

"Well, I... I can't... Please leave me alone!"

"Listen, it's very important. I know she must be upset, but..."

"...She is, actually. Sorry, this is none of my business."

"Where is she?"

"I don't know."

"I think you do. I must speak to her!"

"I can't tell you."

"Of course you can."

"She's gone."

"What do you mean, she's gone?"

"To Africa."

"To Africa? What for? What the hell is she doing there?"

"She's helping the local population."

"I don't understand. Bridget, are you trying to fool me?"

"I'm not, but I've already said too much. I had promised not to tell you anything."

He suddenly looked so sad and desperate.

"This is all my fault", he said wearily.

"I have to go now", she answered.

"All right. Could you just tell me how long she intends to stay there?"

"Three months. The boss agreed to give her a leave immediately."

"She must have been so upset!"

"She loves you. I know I shouldn't but... She's in Tanzania; 'Cross-Cultural Solutions' is the name of the humanitarian organization she's working for."

"Thank you so much, Bridget."

"Actually, I don't know if I've done the right thing, but I think it's so stupid to see two people who love each other being torn apart. I wish you good luck, but please don't hurt her again."

"I won't tell Lea you gave me this piece of information. I don't want her to be angry with you, and I don't mean to hurt her. Have a nice evening. Goodbye, Bridget."

"Goodbye, Alan."

He went back home to search for the address of the organization in England and found out it was based in Brighton. He dialled the number at once.

"Hello, Helen Price for Cross-Cultural Solutions, who's speaking?"

"My name is Alan Wright. I'd like to speak to Lea Norman, in Tanzania. I don't know how to get in touch with her. I have been trying to call her on her mobile phone but I didn't get any answer. There is probably no wireless network in the place where she is. I think you can help me."

"I'm sorry, Mr Wright, there's nothing I can do."

"You must know where she is, and I suppose you've got her address and phone number."

"The thing is, Mr Wright, she asked us not to give you these details."

"But I must speak to her! I desperately need your help."

"I can't help you. The only thing I can suggest is that you write a letter and send it to us. I promise I will pass it on to her without delay. This is the best I can do."

Alan found the situation ridiculous, but it was better than nothing.

"Fine", he answered, "I'll do it. I will send it to you tomorrow. Thank you very much indeed.

Goodbye."

"Goodbye, Mr Wright."

Alan spent a really bad evening. He didn't have dinner. He drank a full glass of whisky, half a gallon of coffee, and smoked a packet of cigarettes. He was thinking of his past with Loreena, their divorce, her accident. When he finally started to write the letter, the only sentence which came to his mind was 'Dear Lea, I love you', which sounded ridiculous. How much did he know about love? How could he assert that he had such a feeling for a woman he had run away from as they were staying in Bruges? He had always been unwilling to move forward as far as feelings had been concerned although in his professional life he had never hesitated. He had just come to realize, at last, that he was a sentimental coward. He had been a successful businessman but his conjugal life had been a complete failure. Could he claim that he had loved his first wife whereas she had been reproaching him for being indifferent, selfish, self-satisfied and scornful, which had led them to a divorce? What about that terrible day when he was supposed to pick up Tina, who was seventeen years old at the time, after a fortnight spent in a holiday camp in Brighton? Business had come first as usual. Instead of postponing a meeting to the next day, he had called Loreena and asked her to fetch their daughter. She had died in a car accident. His children had blamed him then and Tina still did. She had never forgiven him for marrying again shortly after; she had made his life a misery until he broke up with Georgina, his second wife, three years later.

For the first time in his life, he felt responsible for behaving like a coward with the women who had loved him. Time had come for him to face reality, to apologize and hope he would be forgiven instead of starting his letter with stupid words which couldn't make sense unless he proved he did love Lea. He wrote it and sent it the next morning, after a long and restless night. He felt exhausted, suddenly old and useless. The gap between Lea and him seemed to have widened. They were miles apart, and he was frightened; what if she didn't answer his letter? He understood how hard and painful it was to depend on someone's goodwill as surely as he knew he couldn't stand waiting until she was back. He really felt bad at having behaved so foolishly.

On Wednesday afternoon, he called 'Cross-Cultural Solutions' office again to make sure they had received the letter. Helen Price confirmed that she had forwarded it.

"How long will it take for it to reach its destination?" Alan asked.

"Difficult to say. A few days to reach the country. Once in Tanzania, it will take about one week."

"That makes almost a fortnight! It's too long!"

"I'm sorry, Mr Wright. I can't make it shorter."

"Do you realize that if she writes back to me, I won't get her answer before one month?"

"I perfectly do, Mr Wright."

"She might have some internet connection, so it should be possible to send her some messages."

"I'm afraid she doesn't. Shall I remind you that she's working in Africa?"

"Will you give me her address if I take a plane for Tanzania?"

"You know I can't do that!"

"Will you let me fly there without telling me where I can find her?"

"Do as you like, this is not any concern of mine."

Alan was furious, but he couldn't deny that he was reaping what he had sown.

The week passed on very slowly; every morning, when he woke up, Alan wondered what he could do all day long not to get bored to death. He watched TV for hours and had quick meals because he didn't feel like cooking. Sometimes he had a pint of beer or two in a pub, alone. He realized that he had always been far too selfish and, as a result, he was on his own at sixty, learning at last a bit about himself, especially that loneliness was definitely unbearable for him and that without Lea it would be his fate until the end of his life. Was it Lea he desperately needed yet, or just a woman? He had found out in a few days that he had no real friend, nobody he could call any time just to talk for a while. At work as well as in his private life he had never remained on good terms with anybody very long. Lea was his last chance. Why Lea? Why not another woman? Maybe simply because she was his girlfriend and she loved him. He couldn't imagine, anyway, living with a woman his age and getting on in years in her company. He had never thought of Loreena and himself retiring together and playing with their grandchildren like two old fools. He was attracted by young women but he was lucid enough to understand now that he could no longer compare with younger men, that his money had become more attractive than his physique. Lea really loved him; she was kind and honest, and he had to do everything he could not to upset her again, but he couldn't resign himself to staying alone, even for a short period. He needed to be reassured and the only place in the world where he could feel safe was in a woman's arms. On Friday night he called Nicole, his former secretary. He had hired her two years before, she was twenty-eight at the time, quite attractive, and he had had sex with her just as he had started going out with Lea. He invited her for the weekend, which she politely and firmly refused.

"I'm sorry, Alan", she said, "I'm spending the weekend with David, my boyfriend. We're getting married within three months. It's funny you're calling just now; I was actually about to send you an invitation, and I really hope you'll be in at our wedding. David will be happy to meet you." This had been unexpected. The world was marching on and people could still breathe and manage their lives without Alan Wright's consent. Lea was definitely on his mind and he felt ashamed. He understood he shouldn't have called Nicole ; he had just made one more mistake and he knew he shouldn't do that again.

On Saturday morning he visited Heathrow Airport website and booked a seat on the next flight to Dar es Salaam. Two days later he was in Tanzania, a foreigner lost in the 'haven of peace', where he didn't intend to stay. Bagamoyo was his next destination. He knew 'Cross-Cultural Solutions' was very active in this former capital, and he might get a chance to obtain some information about Lea. He spent the night in Dar es Salaam and left the day after, late in the morning. The 45-mile trip was longer than he had expected. The coach was old and slow and the road in poor repair, so that he arrived at Bagamoyo Beach Resort, a French-managed hotel located on the Indian Ocean coast, by the end of the afternoon. Exhausted as he was, he decided it was too late to start investigating; he had a bath, a nice meal, and a walk on the shore before going to bed.

The next morning, he got up early and started for a primary school in which he knew some foreign people were working. Although he hadn't been told which kind of programme Lea had volunteered for, it seemed obvious to him that she couldn't but have chosen to teach. He had some difficulty to find what hardly seemed to be a school, at least for a European. He finally found himself standing in front of a crumbling sort of building. He entered a classroom with neither a door nor windows, only holes instead, and saw a young schoolmistress who was trying to teach young children who only had one English book for six. A few seconds of silence followed his arrival.

"Sorry for interrupting you", he apologized, stepping back.

"It's all right", the young lady answered. "How can I help you?"

"Er... My name is Alan Wright."

"I'm Jennie Brooks. Nice to meet you, Alan."

He was surprised at her being so familiar. Unknown people had always called him 'Mr Wright'!

"Nice to meet you, Miss Brooks. I'm looking for a young English woman, Lea Norman."

"Never heard of her, I'm afraid. You should go and see Bill Parker, an American who works in relation with 'Cross-Cultural Solutions' office."

"Where can I find him?"

"Well, he lives quite a long way from here, actually. You'd better go by bus. I'll show you on the map. Just hang on a second."

The forty children were busy talking and playing now. They didn't pay attention to Alan, except one little girl who came and stood next to him.

"Hello", he said, somewhat amazed at the way she was looking at him.

"Hello", she answered in a quiet voice.

"Do you like school?"

"No."

"No? Why?"

"I don't know."

"School is good. You can learn a lot of things."

"Learn? What for?"

He was about to say 'to have a good job' when he remembered that he wasn't in England. The little girl looked resigned. Jennie was coming back. She had found a plan of Bagamoyo.

"Oh, I see you've met Zahara. She's cute, isn't she?"

"She surely is."

"Look. Here's the school. You must go there, so you'll have to go across the town. Here's his address."

"All right. Is there a bus stop nearby?"

"You'll find a square about two hundred yards from here. Just go this way and wait until the bus arrives."

"Thanks a lot. How long do you think I'll have to wait?"

He realized it was a silly question to ask when he saw Jennie shrug her shoulders.

"OK. I know I'm in Africa."

"So you are. Good luck then. Bye bye."

"Bye bye, Miss Brooks. Bye, Zahara."

The little girl watched him go away, then she looked up and frowned.

Two hours later, he entered a filthy building which happened to be Bill Parker's home. He found a man sitting on a pile of breezeblocks crowned with a wooden board wrapped in some kind of thick fabric, which allowed the whole thing to be comfortable, in the middle of the courtyard.

"Not bad, huh? Well, I know what you think. A kind of aesthetic nonsense! I don't give a damn about what it looks like. My ass appreciates, got it, my friend?"

He was a strange guy. Alan kept silent. How could such a man help him find Lea?

"What are you here for ?Are you gonna help us? You're not the kind, huh?"

"Lea Norman", Alan simply answered.

"Looking for a girl, huh? Lea, you said. Let me think; oh, I remember her."

"Have you met her?"

"Quite a nice girl; nice bottom. Good fuck, my friend, huh?"

Alan turned pale.

"Where is she?"

"Zanzibar."

"Zanzibar? What is she doing there?"

"Teaching, my friend!"

Alan wondered how such a sickening guy could help a humanitarian organization.

"Give me the name of the school, please."

A car stopped outside the building.

"I'll be back in a minute", the man said, and he disappeared.

"Hello, I'm Bill Parker", said someone behind Alan, a few seconds later, "how can I help you?" He turned back.

"Bill Parker?" he asked.

"Yeah. What's the matter? Have you seen a ghost or something?"

"The man who's just left! The one I was talking with before you arrived! He knows Lea, and..."

"Which man? What was he like?"

"About thirty-five, quite tall, fair-haired and..."

"... Particularly rude! Archie Danner! The man was born here, in Tanzania. A few weeks ago, he came and proposed to help me. I soon realized he was a mythomaniac who just wanted to have fun with the young ladies who come over here to work for the organization. He got a particular interest in Lea... Is she the one you've mentioned? Lea Norman?"

"Definitely."

"One evening he got pissed and became disrecpectful to Lea, so I fired him. He disappeared and came back two days ago. I saw him strolling along around here this morning. I don't know what

kind of trouble I'm supposed to expect from him.
Well, that's none of your business, is it? let's talk
about Lea; by the way, are you...?
"Her companion."
"Oh, I see. You're Alan, aren't you?" Before
leaving Bagamoyo, she asked me not to..."
"... Not to tell me where she is, I know that. Look,
Mr Parker, I haven't come all this way to make a
fuss. Lea is angry with me and she's right, but the
only thing I want to do is apologize for my
behaviour, and I hope she'll forgive me."
"I understand but, you know..."
"... Will you let me go back to London without
giving me a chance to see her just for a couple of
hours? I know she's in Zanzibar anyway, unless that
guy told me a lie. Even if you don't tell me where the
school is, I will find it. So please, help me."
"You love her, don't you? All right, I'll give you
her address."
He wrote it on a piece of paper and handed it to
Alan.
"Here it is. Good luck."
"Thanks ever so much, Mr Parker. Oh, just one
more thing, how do I get to Zanzibar?"
"You can go to Dar es Salaam and take the ferry,
or cross by dhow from Bagamoyo. It will take about
five hours."
"What's a dhow?"
"A traditional Arab sailing vessel. If you leave
early tomorrow morning, you'll be at Stone Town
before noon."
'Everything goes so slowly in this country', Alan
said to himself, and he took leave under the

overwhelming sun. He walked back to the spot where he had got off the bus and waited.

"Hi man!", he suddenly heard. He looked over his shoulder and saw Archie Danner.

"Leave me alone!"

"Easy, easy. I guess you've met Mister Bill Parker, huh?"

"Mind your own business. What the hell do you want?"

"Nothing, my friend. Going to Zanzibar? Gonna screw your young lady, huh? Something you have in common with Mister Bill Parker! See you, man." Archie Danner disappeared as quickly as he had come. Alan definitely hated him. Back to the hotel, he asked the receptionist for a phone number.

"A primary school in Zanzibar!"

"Yeah."

"OK. I'll find it out for you."

"I'll be in my room."

Half an hour later, he had a call from the reception. He dialled the number on his cell phone at once, then he hesitated. What if Lea said 'I don't want you to come and see me in Zanzibar. Go back to London'? He decided he'd better go to Stone Town without prior notice.

The next morning, as he was waiting to take on board for the crossing, he met Archie Danner again.

"Hi, my friend. I knew I'd find you here. Have you been thinking of what I told you about Bill Parker and your pretty young lady?"

"You're a liar. Go to hell!"

"You're right about one thing, my friend. Hell is the place where I'll surely end up; but I didn't lie.

I'm a bad man and he's a good one, huh?"

Archie Danner was staring at the skyline. He had lost his arrogance.

"You know, my... What's your name?"

"Alan."

"Archie. You know, Alan, I've done pretty bad things in my life; worse than you can imagine. And I'm a rude man; sure I am! You hate me, Alan. Never mind, I'm used to it."

He kept silent for a while.

"He told me you aggressed Lea and he kicked you off."

"Listen, Alan. There was a party one night and I got pissed as usual. Not only am I rude, but I'm also a heavy drinker, so don't worry, my friend, I won't go to paradise. I didn't aggress Lea the way you imagine. I was just telling her lewd stories, and he got mad at me. Kind of jealous, you know."

"Jealous?"

"Yeah, my friend. That's true he kicked me off, and I kind of fainted behind a hedge at the back of the yard. When I woke up, I don't know how long I had been in a daze, they were together with Lea a few yards from me. All the others had left. She was drunk. I guess he had made her drink to death. She's not the kind, huh?"

"She isn't. She almost never drinks."

"She was on all fours in the grass. What a splendid bottom, man! A delight in the moonlight! He was screwing her. A hard fuck, my friend, I dare say."

"No more details, please!"

"I guess you're upset, aren't you?"

"Sure I am. Was it only a matter of sex?"

"It was nothing but sex. He wanted some more, but when she recovered from boozing, some time later, she refused. She said 'no, Bill, it won't happen again."

"What did he say?"

"Nothing much. He just said it wasn't fair to leave him with such a hard-on, and he tried to fuck her again. She was furious and called him a 'mother-fucker'. He called her a 'bitch' in return. I don't think they have met again ever since."

"Why are you telling me all that?"

"Because I like you, Alan."

"How do I know you aren't lying?"

"Ask Lea. Tell her I said everything to you. She's an honest girl, she won't lie. Listen, Alan, let me give you a good piece of advice. Take her away from here, go back to London as soon as you can and forget about it all!"

"A wise man, huh?"

They both laughed happily at such a remark.

Six hours later, Alan was standing in front of the school, worried. He had been looking forward to that moment; he had felt quite excited during the crossing, at least at the beginning. He was apprehensive about seeing Lea again. He could hear children singing a song; he didn't understand Swahili, but it sounded good. He waited until they had a break. A flow of kids hurried outside, and two African schoolmistresses came to meet him.

"Hello", he said, a little apologizingly, "I'm Alan Wright, Lea's companion. I would like to speak to her."

The two women looked at each other with embarrassment.

"Hello, I'm Baako, and this is Machupa."

"Nice to meet you... Is Lea around?"

"I'm afraid she isn't", Baako answered.

"Well, I think she teaches in this school, doesn't she?"

"She's not in today."

"Where is she, then?"

"We don't know. She said she wouldn't come for a few days."

"All right. She lives somewhere, doesn't she?"

"We don't know where she lives."

It seemed obvious that they were lying. Alan understood that someone had told Lea about his visit.

"Who told her?" he asked.

"What do you mean? Machupa asked.

"Who told her I was coming here? Who called her?"

"I don't know", Machupa answered.

"You do know! Did Lea tell you she didn't want to see me? Of course she did!"

"She's afraid of you!" Baako went on.

"Baako, are you afraid of me? Do I look so frightening?"

"No, sir", they both answered.

"Was it Bill Parker who called her? Archie Danner, maybe?"

"Mr Parker", Baako admitted, "he said you were very angry about what Mr Danner told you."

"Listen." Alan sat down. "I'm not angry. What Mr Danner told me didn't make me angry."

"But you've threatened Mr Parker, and you hit him", Machupa went on.

"I didn't hit or threaten anybody, I swear. That man is a bloody liar. Lea is wrong if she believes him. I want to speak to her, that's all."

Baako and Machupa looked at each other again. They didn't know what to say. A long minute passed. They were standing motionless in front of Alan who was staring at the wooden floor. All this fortunately came to an end when Lea appeared in the corridor leading to the classrooms. She was walking slowly. She was almost crying. Alan stood up and opened his arms.

"Lea! At last! Come and see me, my baby. Don't be afraid."

She did so and he started cuddling her.

"Oh, my Lea! I'm so sorry."

They went out for a walk, both impatient to talk.

"Alan, I don't know what Archie Danner told you about Bill Parker..."

"... And you? He told me what happened."

"I shouldn't have done such a thing. I was drunk, you know, and..."

"Forget it."

"I just can't! Do you think it's so easy? I need you to forgive me. I feel so guilty!"

Alan felt hurt. His male pride had been offended but it was his fault, the consequence of his selfish behaviour.

"You needn't be forgiven, Lea. All that would never have happened if I hadn't been so stupid. I've come here to apologize and ask you to come and live with me. I love you; I really do."

Several minutes of shared emotion followed. They had reached the beach by then and sat on a bench.

"Do you really want us to live together?"

"Did you read my letter?"

"I got no letter from you."

"Never mind; I don't want to live away from you any more."

"That's so unexpected!"

"You know, Archie Danner gave me a nice piece of advice. I had never thought I would give credence to the opinion of such a man. He's not so bad, in fact."

"He's been nice to me."

"And all he said to me was true."

"What did he advise you to do?"

"Well, I can't tell you everything he said. You know how rude he can be, don't you?"

"It must be his own way to make people think he's worse than he seems to be."

"Probably... He advised me to take you back to London!"

"I don't know, Alan."

"Do you love me?"

"Of course I do, but I've got to think about it."

"I understand it's hard to believe an old fool like me, but I promise we'll organize ourselves as soon as you're back home, if you agree."

"How long will you stay here?"

"Maybe a few days. I mean, in Bagamoyo. I won't stay in Stone Town if that bothers you. I can leave now if you want me to."

She looked at him in wonder. A new and wiser

man he seemed to be. More loving and sensitive too. She looked at him with tenderness.

"Don't you want me to show you around my place?"

"That would be nice indeed."

"I'll go back to the school to help my colleagues, then I'll take you there and you'll stay with me tonight."

Alan didn't answer. He didn't have to. Lea's proposal wasn't to be discussed.

They spent a wonderful evening together, as if they had come to Stone Town for a honeymoon, in a light and peaceful atmosphere. Lea had the next day off so that they could have a long lie-in, then a nice bath in the sea before Alan boarded a dhow for Bagamoyo. She had finally agreed to go back to London earlier than expected. Yet she wouldn't leave Tanzania before somebody had replaced her. A new girl was to arrive ten days later, so plans were settled for Lea to leave the country soon after.

"I'll be in London in about a fortnight, Alan."

"That's fine. I'll pick you up at the airport."

"All right."

"OK. I'm looking forward to it."

Alan returned to London two days later. He was both lost after the change of scenery his stay in Tanzania had involved, and happy about his love relationship with Lea. Now he had a realistic view of his future life with her. He would allow her to bring some furniture and all kinds of personals to his house. He had decided to clear away all the stuff he had gathered in a spare room which looked like a pigsty. He started working on it right away. He took a lot of things to the rubbish dump and washed the floor, then he considered the poor condition of the wallpaper and thought he had to change it. He steamed it off and went to a store to choose some new one, a task he soon proved unable to achieve without somebody's advice.

He invited Tina and Tom's family for lunch at the weekend, and profited by the occasion to tell them Lea was to come and live with him shortly. They were amazed indeed. Alan glanced at his daughter who didn't look so happy about the news.

"Tina, do you have anything against Lea?" he asked her.

"Nothing at all. You know it, don't you?"

"I think I do, as well as I know that you don't approve of our union. She should be with a younger man, shouldn't she? You see, Tina, the truth is that I love her, and she loves me."

He told them about Bagamoyo and Zanzibar, Stone Town and the primary school, without giving unnecessary details indeed. Tina was moved.

"You didn't think your father could have any positive feelings, did you?" he carried on, addressing her. She looked flabbergasted.

"Don't look at me as if you had seen a ghost. You were probably right and I can't blame you for judging me so severely."

He broke off for a short while, then he went on.

"Just one more thing, Tina. Would you do me a favour ?"

"Sure. What is it?"

"It's about the wallpaper in the spare room next to my office. I'd like to change it, but I need your advice, so if you accepted to come with me to the store and…"

Tina started laughing.

"I wasn't trying to be funny," he said.

"I know, Dad, but that's so unexpected! It's all right, I'll do my best to help you."

"Unexpected! I think I heard it a few days ago! Thanks a lot, I really appreciate."

"I think Lea will really appreciate too," Hanna replied.

"I hope she will. I don't want her to be disappointed."

Tina actually went to a wallpaper shop with her father the day after. They hadn't spent much time together for ages; most of the talks they had had in the recent years had been arguments. Even if there wasn't a deep bond between them yet, something close to complicity made them both enjoy their afternoon search and the cup of coffee they had in a nearby café.

Back home, Alan started to put up the wallpaper they had chosen. By Thursday he had finished working in the room. Lea was to arrive at Heathrow Airport on Friday morning, by twenty-five past six.

Lea was aboard the dhow from Zanzibar to Bagamoyo. She was waving goodbye to Baako, Machupa, and a group of children who were all sorry to see her off. Of course she had promised to come back soon although she knew that she most probably wouldn't. When they eventually became tiny creatures gesturing on the beach, she sat down and started to think of the day when Alan had left her alone in Bruges. After reading his letter, she had hated him from the bottom of her heart. She had been overcome by anger. When she had arrived in London, the day after, she had understood that she had to stay out of reach of him. She had to leave.

She had remembered a young woman she had known a couple of years before, who had left her job temporarily to work for a humanitarian organization in Africa for six months, so she had got in touch with 'Cross-Cultural Solutions'. They needed someone in Tanzania without delay, so she had asked permission for leave from her boss who had agreed to let her go. All the details of her departure had been settled rapidly. She had made her decision in the middle of the week and taken the plane for Dar es Salaam on the following Sunday.

Lea had had no news from Alan before leaving and was quite relieved by his silence which, on the other hand, had made her hate him even more. She remembered her tears at the airport and the hardship it had been to fit into Tanzanian life. Bill Parker had been very welcoming and had pretended to take her under his wing during the two weeks she had spent in Bagamoyo. Archie Danner had frightened her though he had never tried to harm her. She had been deeply mistaken about both of them and still couldn't forgive herself for having sex with a bastard like Parker. She had never been unfaithful to any man before, and although it could by no means be asserted that she had been to Alan, as he had broken up with her, she thought of it as a stain in their relation. Until she learnt that Alan had tried to get in touch with her, she had seen the matter as an event of no importance, whereas she had been feeling guilty as soon as she had heard that he had set foot on the Tanzanian soil, especially as it was Bill Parker himself who had told her on the phone, lying shamelessly to her.

"Hello, Lea, it's Bill. How are you?"

" ... "

"Fine? All right. Still O.K. with the school?"

" ... "

"Well, Sweetie, let me tell you... Well, quite an embarrassing piece of news, actually."

" ... "

"It's about Alan Wright, you know."

" ... "

"Yes, he is."

" ... "

"What do you mean, where ? Here, in Bagamoyo. He came to see me, and made such a fuss! He swung at me like a wild beast!"

" ... "

"Why? Because he knows about us. Archie Danner, that fucking bastard, told him and sent him to me. I had to tell him you're in Stone Town."

" ... "

"Lea, he would've killed me if I hadn't! Sure he would!"

" ... "

"Stay away from the school for a few days. Your colleagues will say they don't know where you live. Why don't you go and visit Pemba? A nice opportunity, huh?"

She hadn't followed his advice; she hadn't stayed away from the school because she wanted to know what she would feel like seeing him again. Then she had known how guilty, how ashamed she was feeling, and above all how much she loved him.

She got off the dhow by noon. Her large bulging rucksack and her big suitcase were heavy. She was pacing slowly towards the town, hoping to find a bus which would take her to the hotel where Alan had been staying. Beads of sweat were rolling down her pretty face. She was wiping her forehead when she saw Archie Danner getting into an old Peugeot car a few yards away from her.

"Archie!" she called.

He raised his eyes and caught sight of her.

"Fucking hell! What are you doing here, sweet baby?"

"I'm going home!"

"Bloody good news! Gonna have a hell of fun with your old boy, huh? "Well, tell me what I can do for you. Give you a lift somewhere?"

She explained that she was on the way to Bagamoyo Beach Resort and expected to leave for Dar es Salaam the day after, as early as possible, to catch her plane.

"Give me your luggage, then. Let me take you to the hotel, then to the airport tomorrow."

"It's ever so nice of you, Archie. Thanks ever so much."

"It's all right. Come on, sweet baby, let's go!"

He found his way through the busy streets of the town. When they reached their destination, Lea was in a sweat; She was desperate for a shower. It was madness not to drive an air-conditioned car in that country. Archie carried her luggage into the entrance of the hotel and promised he would be back by nine the next morning.

He actually was. Lea was to take the plane at half past five in the afternoon, so she had to be at the airport by half past three.

"Don't worry", Archie said as they were leaving the town, "We have plenty of time. You won't be late, baby, you can trust me."

"I trust you, Archie, but I'm not sure I can trust that old banger."

"It never breaks down. You'd better think that tomorrow morning, at this time, you'll be French kissing good old Alan!"

"Oh, Archie!"

"Oh, Archie! Take it easy, baby doll, you know Archie is an awful joker, huh?"

"And a good man!"

Archie looked uncomfortable.

"No matter what I am, or what I'm not. I'm driving a pretty swell girl on the road to happiness, and I like it."

In spite of Lea's fear, they reached Dar es Salaam without any trouble. She had plenty of time before checking her luggage, so she invited Archie for lunch.

"Have a nice trip, sweet baby", he said when time had come to say goodbye, "Say hello to my friend, Alan. How bloody lucky he is! Tell him he should marry you, and if he doesn't I will!"

"You're so funny! Come over to London some time."

"Good idea, I'd like to see with my own eyes if the Gherkin really fucks the clouds."

"Oh, Archie!"

They embraced good-humouredly, then Lea went to the check-in desk. She queued up with the other passengers, then called Alan a few minutes before boarding-time. After the plane had taken off, she thought of their relationship, of Alan's fear of being seen as too old a man to be with a young woman. She wondered whether he would be scared at the idea of becoming her children's father. She was seriously thinking of having a baby, which she had never considered before. As Alan had insisted to welcome her in his house, he might be happy about having a child then. He wasn't a cradle snatcher and she was neither a gold digger nor a sugar baby. They dearly loved each other, so founding a family could naturally stem from their love. Remembering Archie's words, she even caught herself hoping that Alan would propose to marry her.

When the plane landed at Heathrow Airport in the morning mist, she called Alan again. It was about quarter past ten when she threw herself into his arms. They left the airport, French kissing as the mist was getting thicker.

"You look good!" she said tenderly as he was driving towards Richmond.

"I'm so happy you're back at last, Lea. I love you."

She leant her head on his shoulder, her eyes half-closed.

"Are you tired?"

"A little.

"I'll prepare a nice breakfast for you, then you'll have a rest if you wish."

"I'll have plenty of time to rest; I'll have a week off before going back to work."

They arrived at Alan's house soon. He stopped his car opposite the street.

"Stay in the car while I open the gate. I'll park inside."

"Let me open it. You'll just have to drive in, all right?"

"All right. Give me a kiss."

They kissed before she crossed the street and opened the gate. She was about to turn back when she heard a screech of brakes preceding the awful kind of noise one hears when a car bumps into another. She stood petrified in front of the garden entrance, a young woman full of hope for happiness suddenly paralyzed by fear.

A lorry seemed to have swallowed the car. Alan was leaning motionless against the steering wheel.

THE TEACHER

The French lesson was over; the pupils were going out of the classroom. Gary was about to leave when Sarah, a fourteen-year-old blue-eyed brunette, came up to him and handed him an envelope.

"Sir, it's from my mother", she said.

"Thank you, Sarah."

He opened it and started reading.

Martha Spencer
28 Liddon Road
BR1 Bromley

Monday, October 19th

Sir,

I feel a little worried concerning Sarah's grades in French. Although they are not bad indeed, I dare say they are less good this year than they used to be during her first three years in this school. I'd like to make an appointment with you before half-term. Any time after 5 o'clock would suit me fine.

Thank you in anticipation for your answer.

Martha Spencer

He had a strange feeling when he looked up and met her eyes; large light-blue eyes staring at him questioningly.

"Tomorrow evening", he declared, "at quarter past five; do you think it will suit your mother?"

"I think so", Sarah answered, "Let me write it down in my notebook... Tuesday, October 20th, quarter past five. That's O.K. Thank you very much, sir."

"You're welcome."

"Bye, sir."

"Bye, Sarah."

Gary had been teaching in Bromley for fifteen years. His parents, who had both retired recently, had been French teachers as well. Speaking Racine's language had become a trademark in the family. Gary's wife herself spoke French, as her own mother was from Dunkerque. She had settled in England and married an English ophthalmologist.

Although all these people were fond of spending time in France, especially in the summer, none of them really enjoyed the French way of life.

Jennie was already back home, having a cup of tea, when he stepped into the living-room.

"Hello, darling, did you have a nice day at work?"

"Beautiful day! What about your teaching business?"

"All right. Any great piece of news?"

"Nothing except a phone call from Mum."

"How is she?"

"Perfectly fine."

"What about your Dad?"

"Making fun of the French, as usual."

"As long as he can laugh at the expense of French people, anyway, you'll never have to worry about his health. What about Bobby and Beverley?"

"Bob is busy doing his homework. As for Beverley, she looked sullen when she came in."

"She probably got a bad grade; a mere 'A' whereas she expected 'A plus', if not 'A double plus'! She's like that!"

"I don't think so; she would have told me. Half-term will be most welcome; she looks tired."

Beverley was ten years old. She was dark-haired with large light blue eyes, an excellent pupil who was never satisfied with her results, which worried her parents insofar as she was rarely happy. Bobby, who was two years older, was quite a different character. He did his homework seriously, got quite good grades and was never stressed about anything.

Later, during dinner, Gary asked Beverley what had been going wrong during the day. He got no immediate answer. She just shrugged and looked up at him as if to say 'I just can't tell you. Too hard to say!' Later, as Bobby had gone for a bath, Jennie insisted.

"It's about Charlotte", Beverley admitted.

Charlotte and she had been best friends since nursery school.

"Her father left yesterday. She cried all day long."

"Do you mean he left for good?" Jennie asked.

"He did, mum. He will never come back."

"We understand that you're upset", Gary said, "if there's anything we can do... For instance, if Charlotte wants to come and spend the weekend with us..."

"No, dad. It wouldn't help her. It's so unfair, she doesn't deserve it."

Beverley sounded angry.

"Nobody deserves it; it's very unfortunate that it happened to Charlotte, but you must know that her father and her mother didn't get on any more."

"I know that, dad, but I'm sad. I feel so sorry for Charlotte."

The next morning, she got up earlier than usual.

"Morning, dad", she said to her father who was about to leave, "give me a kiss."

Gary took her in his arms and kissed her goodbye.

"Why did you get up so early?" her mother asked from the kitchen.

"I'm going to Charlotte's house to pick her up there."

Every morning, Beverley left home when Mark, the next door neighbours' son, came and stood on the pavement in front of her parents' house until she turned up outside. They walked about three hundred yards and met Charlotte and her mother at the crossroads; then the three schoolchildren walked on to the school which happened to be located a quarter of a mile further down the road.

"Will Mark go to Charlotte's with you?"

"Yes, mum, don't worry."

Gary and Jennie would by no means have considered positively that their daughter might be alone in the street in the early morning.

"Mark is such a nice boy, mum. I suggested that he came with me and he accepted at once."

"He's got excellent manners!"

"Let's hope he will never change. I wish Charlotte's father were like him!"

"Listen, Beverley! I know what you're feeling like, but you must remember what dad told you last night. Help your friend as much as you can, but don't you judge her father; it will bring you nothing but sorrow."

"You're probably right, mum. I'll do my best."

"All right, darling. Now you must have breakfast."

"O.K. Where's Bobby?"

"He's been in the bathroom for almost twenty minutes!"

"Is he admiring himself in the mirror?" Beverley asked, laughing.

"He most probably is."

"He's in love with Samantha Jenkins!"

"How do you know that?"

"It's a secret, mum."

"A secret? Well, finish your breakfast and kick him out of the bathroom."

"Do you like Samantha Jenkins?"

"I do like her, she's very nice; as for you, Beverley, stop talking and talking and talking..."

"Got it, mum. I've almost finished."

Bobby came downstairs just as Beverley was coming out of the kitchen.

"Oh, that's unfair, Bobby. I was supposed to kick you out of the bathroom!"

"You won't, nasty sister of mine! And stop telling lies! I'm not in love with Samantha Jenkins."

"I know you are!"

"Oh, shut up. See you later, mum."

"See you later, son."

"See you later, Piggy."

"Don't ever call me Piggy again!"

"Don't ever tell anybody I'm in love with Samantha again!"

"All right, brother!"

Ten minutes later, Mark was outside, waiting for Beverley.

"There is Mark, Darling, hurry up", Jennie urged her daughter.

"I'm ready. Kiss, mum."

"Kiss, darling. See you in the afternoon."

"See you, mum."

A few hours later, at the end of the school day, Gary was feeling exhausted. He was sitting in the staff room, drinking coffee. He still had to meet Mrs Spencer, hoping it wouldn't last long. He took his teacher's book out of his briefcase and compared Sarah's grades with those of the whole class. 'Nothing alarming', he thought, 'I hardly understand why Mrs Spencer is worried. She must be an anxious mother who needs to be reassured'. Five minutes later, he was heading for room 11, where teachers and parents could talk privately, when he caught sight of the silhouette of a woman at the end of the corridor. She was walking gracefully, just like... Martha... Martha Henley! How could that be possible? Almost fifteen years, already!

"Hello, Gary", she said when they found themselves standing face to face.

"Martha?"

"I understand that you are surprised."

"I must admit... Well, I didn't expect... So you are Martha Spencer now."

"I've actually been Martha Spencer for fourteen years. I married Harry, the headmaster of the school

I'm still teaching in, two months after Sarah's birth."

"Let's go in", he answered, nodding towards room 11. He opened the door to let her in. It was furnished with a table and four chairs. He offered her a seat.

"So you'd like us to talk about Sarah's results, wouldn't you?"

"Yes, indeed."

"Honestly, I don't think you have any reason to be worried. She's quite a good pupil; her grades may not match up to your expectations, or hers, but I am personally quite satisfied."

"It's all right then. I just wanted to have your opinion about her abilities in French."

"They're quite good."

They talked a lot about Sarah's attitude in class, how self-effaced she was, her evident shyness, until Martha changed the subject.

"So, what about you?"

"What do you mean?"

"I know you're married and you have two children, Bobby and Beverley, don't you?"

Gary frowned.

"You haven't come here just to talk about Sarah's results, have you?"

"I loved you so much, Gary!"

"We used to love each other, Martha, but I have Jennie, Bobby and Beverley whereas you've got your husband and Sarah. By the way, does she have any brother or sister?"

"Sarah is our single child. My single child, I mean. My husband is sterile. She's my daughter as well as yours!"

Gary frowned again.

"Shall I remind you that she's fourteen? You left me exactly eight months before she was born."

Gary remembered almost fearfully that they had broken up in December 1994.

"Sarah was born in August 1995, wasn't she? Why didn't you tell me?"

"Do you really think it would have prevented you from leaving me? It wasn't worth trying to make you stay."

"All that's wrong, as you know it! You were the one who wanted to break up. I wasn't!"

"You're lying, Gary", Martha answered quietly.

"I'm not! What the hell do you want?"

"There's no need to be aggressive. I'd like to talk with you, that's all!"

"What's the need?"

"Well, Gary. What does it matter whether I broke up or you did?"

"There's nothing much to talk about then, apart from the fact that Sarah might be my daughter."

"She definitely is!"

"So what? I understand she's been legally recognized by your husband, hasn't she?"

"She has, but she doesn't know that he isn't her biological father."

"The less she knows the better. If she's happy as she is, she doesn't have to know I'm her father, if ever I am."

"I swear you are!"

"All right, Martha. I think this conversation is over."

"When shall we talk, Gary?"

"Come on, Martha! We've been talking."

"Do you really want to know why I didn't tell you I was pregnant? This was your own question, wasn't it?"

Before he had time to answer, she went on.

"When I started feeling that you were about to leave me, I had such a hard time! I accepted that I should live without you, but I wanted to keep a link with you; the indestructible link that still unites two people years and years after they've parted, even after death. I desperately wished I would get pregnant anyway; and I did."

Martha had a sort of light in her eyes as she was speaking which made Gary think that she had become a maniac. The frightening thought was that she might have been so for at least fifteen years and was likely to remain so until the end of her days, which by all means could be fraught with serious consequences considering that if she had recently decided, as the inevitable result of the evolution of a possible mental disease, to make his life a hell, whatever conscious or not her purpose might be, he wasn't out of the woods yet.

Martha had met Harry Spencer on Thursday, September 1st, on the train from Reading to London. She had just been appointed as a teacher in North East London. She was twenty-five, a tall, attractive young woman with long dark hair. Harry was sitting opposite her, reading some notes from a speech he was to make later in the morning in front of the staff of a secondary school in Hackney. He was thirty-five, a stern-looking man.

"Nice weather", he had suddenly declared, looking up to her. He didn't sound self-confident.

She had liked it.

"Very nice indeed."

"Do you live in Reading?" he had ventured to ask.

"I don't, actually. I've been visiting my parents. I live in London."

"Do you? I live in Reading with my wife. We've been married for seven years."

"Have you? Do you have children?"

"Unfortunately we don't", he had answered painfully.

Martha had started feeling uneasy. She had regretted having asked such a question.

"I'm sorry... I..."

"It's all right", he had answered, going back to his notes to put an end to their conversation.

When the newly appointed headmaster, whom everybody in the school knew as he had been deputy head for two years before, had entered the assembly hall, Martha had cried out in surprise. Harry Spencer had started speaking with great confidence, capturing his colleagues' attention, a shy man in private life addressing the audience with authority.

"Listen, Martha", Gary concluded, "you'd better go home now, and let Sarah go her own way. Your family and mine are happy, so don't make the situation complicated."

"O.K. then. I'm going back home. See you again!" she answered in a way that made him fear that trouble might come soon.

"I'm glad to see you again", Harry Spencer had declared when she had been introduced to him after the assembly, "I didn't expect to see you here, I'm so happy."

For a second or two, he had seemed to lose his self-confidence, then remembering that he was the headmaster, he had regained his composure.

Martha had understood straight away that Harry was irresistibly attracted, which had been borne out soon by the fact that he missed no opportunity to see her either in the staff room or along the corridors or in his office. She hadn't said much about herself in the first place but she had encouraged him to talk about himself so that she had come to know quite a great deal about his life.

At that time, Harry was Sheila's husband. The first two years of their conjugal life had been quite happy. Sheila had received from him the kind of peaceful comfort she had always expected from a man and was flattered that 'such a brilliant mind', as she often said, might become a school headmaster pretty soon. Their relationship had begun to deteriorate when he had started getting more and more involved in his job. Feeling neglected, she had expressed her wish to have a child. Harry had happily agreed but one year later she was still not pregnant. The fertility tests she had undergone were positive, so they had tried another six months, still unsuccessfully. She had begun to wonder whether her husband might be sterile, an assumption he had hardly coped with until he had been forced to accept it. He had become dismal whereas Sheila, disappointed, had been more and more distant. He had proposed to adopt a child but she had refused, arguing that she felt like bearing her own baby; in vitro fertilization didn't work, so she got more and more depressed.

One day, by mid-January 1995, Harry asked Martha in for a drink. They went to a nearby pub and ordered two pints of beer.

"Harry", for they had come into the habit of calling each other by their Christian names when talking privately, "I thought you never drank alcohol!" she pointed out.

"Let's sit over there", he answered, seemingly ignoring her remark, "and let me tell you something really important."

They sat and she waited until he spoke again. He took a sip of beer first.

"Well, Martha, you're the only person... I mean..."

'He has something to say about his wife, I'm sure', she reflected, 'I can feel this kind of thing. If he tells me she has moved on to another man, I'll be a little sad for him but I'll be so happy for myself. Let him tell me he will divorce, and I promise he'll sleep in my bed tonight!'

"Sheila and I broke up just after Christmas. She moved out on New year's Eve. I'm alone now."

"Gary and I broke up too."

"Did you?"

"We did, a few days before Christmas."

"It's very unfortunate indeed. I'm sorry!"

"Well, it's not so bad, really. Look, Harry, we're both alone, all right, but we are together, aren't we?"

He replied in a mumble she couldn't understand.

"Harry, why do you think we are here in this pub, telling each other about our misfortunes? Tell me, honestly."

"We are best friends."

"Are we best friends by chance?"

"Maybe we aren't."

She expected him to say something like 'it's a sure sign we are meant to become even closer', take another sip and declare straight out 'I love you, Martha'. As he didn't, she decided to take the bull by the horns.

"Are you going back to Reading tonight?"

"I'm supposed to take the 18.58 train, as I usually do."

"This is what you're supposed to do, but you don't have to. Nobody's waiting for you there. Why don't you stay in London, with me? Come to my place and I'll prepare a nice meal, just for us and..." She lowered her eyes. "You must think that's all so rude of me!"

"Of course not."

"Are you sure? Maybe I'm a little tight, but since we met I've had the feeling that you and I..." She looked down again, with pretended shyness.

"I love you, Martha", Harry uttered all of a sudden.

Martha looked up at him with a broad smile on her face. He had plucked the courage to say it at last.

"Oh, Harry!"

"I've been in love with you since we met on the train."

They actually had dinner at Martha's; Harry didn't go back to Reading that evening. As weeks passed he stayed in London more and more often. He soon learnt that Martha was pregnant, which would allow him to be a father if they ever got married, and was happy to know that she had no desire to have more than one child. Sarah was born during the summer holidays and the wedding took place in October.

As for Gary, he had fallen in love with a pleasant young lady who worked as a midwife at the Princess Royal University Hospital. They had been introduced at a party given by one of his colleagues whose wife had made friends with Jennie when their first daughter had been born. They had met every day ever since that night, had been on holiday together, to France indeed. They got married in July 1996, in Dunkerque to please Jennie's mother.

Remembering his first meeting with his wife, his marriage, their children's birth, but also the three years he had spent with Martha, he was driving home, worried about possibly being Sarah's father. Luckily enough, Jennie was working the nine-to-nine shift that day and would be back home late, presumably exhausted, they wouldn't have time to talk very long so that she wouldn't realize how tense he was, she would fall asleep soon and maybe he would feel better in the morning. It was the first time he had been happy not to see her at home after a day's work. Most of all, he didn't want her to be worried; he had to protect her as well as their children who might be as anxious as Sarah if they learnt the truth. He had felt that Martha wouldn't mind taking Jennie away from him and was ready to use whatever means she could to reach her goal. Nevertheless he couldn't rule out that she might have been lying just in order to frighten him. Why then would she have done such a thing? He really didn't know what to think. He was so disconcerted.

He parked his car in front of the garage and

entered the house. Bobby was coming down the stairs.

"Hello, dad! Nice day at school?"

This was his everyday joke, except when something had been going wrong.

"Hello, son! Nice day at school?"

This was Gary's everyday answer, except when he was supposed to inquire about what had been going wrong.

"Where's your sister?"

"She's upstairs, homeworking in her bedroom."

"O.K. I'll see her in a minute."

Gary went into the living-room and flopped into an armchair. He felt like having a drink, just like some of his friends, when the school day was over. Jack and Daniel, an English and a History teacher, were used to having a glass of Dimple or Aberlour every afternoon, from Monday to Friday. On Saturday nights, at the pub, they drank deer. Gary had a pint or two with them about once a month, when Jennie could join them.

He had to see Beverley first. He climbed up the stairs and was about to knock at her door when she opened it.

"Hello, dad. Give me a kiss?"

"Of course, my baby daughter."

"I'm not your baby daughter any more. I'm a grown-up little girl."

"Ah, grown-up but little! Quite a paradox, isn't it? What am I supposed to call you now?"

"Just call me... Well... Let me think..."

While uttering these words, she was staring at him with large light-blue eyes...

"Dad, are you listening to me?"

... Just like Sarah's.

"Dad?"

"Excuse me, Beverley, I..."

"Have you seen a ghost? Hey dad, it's me. I'm your daughter!"

"I'm sorry. I just don't feel very well, you know. I think I'd better have a rest before dinner."

"All right, I'm going back to my homework then."

"Good girl! See you later."

Downstairs, he stopped all of a sudden. He had just seen his reflection in the large mirror and realized that Sarah's eyes as well as Beverley's were the very image of his. He sat on the second step and went on watching his own face for a while. No doubt Martha had told him the truth.

He was no longer thinking of drinking any alcohol. He would prepare something good for dinner and try to look as relaxed as possible. He would even try to joke with his children.

He actually did so. When Jennie came home, he had recollected himself enough not to make her believe something unpleasant had possibly occurred. Three days passed; he felt uncomfortable indeed having to be faced with Sarah at school, but he did his best not to meet her eyes. The half-term holidays came at the right time. He spent the first four days with Bobby and Beverley at home while their mother was busy at the hospital, then he took them to his parents' on Wednesday. They were to stay there until Saturday, a period which was off for Jennie, so that Gary and she allowed themselves to some romantic time on their own. They had chosen the Isle of Wight as a destination because it wasn't too far from London and neither of them had ever been there. They were to leave early enough on Thursday morning to be in Portsmouth for the eleven o'clock outward crossing. As Bobby had recently destroyed their only travel bag, they mainly had suitcases, during a two-day school trip, they decided to go to the Glades Shopping Centre and buy a new one. They had parked at the Mall, Elmfield Road, and were walking past Marks and Spencer's when a lady called Gary. He turned round, amazed.

"Mr Blackstone!"

He had almost forgotten Martha since the beginning of the holidays, then she was there, standing in front of him.

"Mrs... Spencer! ... What a surprise!"

"I'm so glad to see you again, Mr Blackstone!"

"Mrs Spencer", Gary continued, a little shyly, "this is Jennie, my wife!" He had insisted on the last two words, stressing them to make her understand that he wanted to be left alone with his own family.

"I'm delighted, Mrs Blackstone."

"Nice to meet you, Mrs Spencer", Jennie answered in a neutral voice.

"Well", Gary went on, "we've got some shopping to do. Have a nice afternoon!"

"Same to you. I hope to see you again soon, Mr Blackstone!"

Martha sounded self-confident and looked quite satisfied. Gary didn't like her attitude.

"Is this the woman you had an appointment with last Tuesday?" Jennie asked as they were entering the shopping centre.

"She actually is", Gary sighed.

"She seems to impress you, doesn't she?"

"I'm not impressed. I'm only worried about the way she behaves with her daughter."

"Are you? Is she a possessive mother?"

"Maybe."

"Is Sarah a nice girl?"

"She really is... By the way, how do you know her name? I didn't tell you, did I?"

"I think you did. How could I know?"

"I'm wondering... Well, I must have told you, otherwise you wouldn't... Yet I don't remember telling you..."

"Let's forget about it. It doesn't matter at all, does it?"

"I guess it doesn't."

They went into a shop and chose a travel bag, then they had a walk around, window-shopping for a while, before drove back home.

They were at Gunwharf, Portsmouth harbour, quite on time the day after. Once at Fishbourne, Gary drove towards Ryde, then he followed the road signs to Sandown.

"Would you please have a look at the map, love?" he asked Jennie. "I don't remember where I have to turn off."

"All right. Let me see... Well, you'll turn off for St Helens, then you'll drive down to Bembridge. The hotel is located past the lifeboat station."

"Thanks a lot. Wonderful view, isn't it? We're so lucky the sky is cloudless."

"It should be so for the next couple of days."

"Fine! Shall we have a snack at the coffee lounge when we get there? I wouldn't mind a ploughman's lunch with a pint of beer."

"Hopefully, but I'd like to see our room first."

It was a beautifully designed room overlooking the Solent, with a large and luxurious bed, a personal mini bar and an en suite bathroom. Jennie was delighted; Gary had in mind their meeting with Martha the day before and he was already thinking of their return on the mainland with some apprehension. Nevertheless he had decided to make the most of their short stay on the isle, hoping that Jennie wouldn't mention Martha, which she took great care not to do.

After lunch, they left for Osborne House, a former royal residence in Cowes. They visited the Durbar Room with its stunning decor, the opulent private apartments including the Queen's bedroom, nursery rooms and royal bathrooms, the Swiss Cottage, then strolled around the extensive grounds.

"Marvellous gardens!" Gary pointed out, I understand why Queen Victoria loved this place."

"My parents too: Mum was so happy when I told her we intended to come over here, at last."

"At last! This is what your father said to me. He loves this place, indeed."

Jennie's parents had met on the Isle of Wight forty-three years earlier. Claire, her mother, who was twenty-two, was visiting England with Annie, a French friend. Andrew, her father, had spotted her during the crossing, but he had been too shy to walk up to her. Claire hadn't even noticed him, but her friend had. Later, in East Cowes, Andrew had caught sight of the two young ladies again and had decided to leave the group of boys he was with to follow them. Annie had turned round to smile at him several times, so he had started a conversation with her. She was staring hungrily at him whereas he only had eyes for Claire.

"Poor Annie, what a hard time it must have been for her. After that, mum didn't hear of her for ten years! She felt so humiliated, so upset!"

"Well, your parents had done nothing wrong, except falling in love with each other. Your father told me a hundred times how romantic their first kiss had been."

"One morning, he invited my mother to visit Osborne House, which she accepted, and when Annie she saw them walking hand in hand later in the afternoon, she was so angry she left without delay. Mum certainly felt embarrassed, but she obviously got over it fast and stayed with dad until the end of his stay, and I know they had their first night together here!"

"Your father didn't tell me about that!"

"Mum told me!"

"Well, let's have a kiss, right here, then we'll have our first romantic night on the Isle of Wight."

As Gary was taking Jennie in his arms, his telephone rang. He saw their phone number displayed on the screen. Before leaving, he had diverted their home calls to his mobile phone.

"Hello, Gary Blackstone speaking."

"Hello, Mr Blackstone."

He stepped away from Jennie and frowned.

"Who's speaking?"

"Martha, of course. You can't imagine how glad I was to see you yesterday. What about having dinner one evening? Shall we say next week? I mean, you and I!"

"I'm sorry. I'm not mister Blackpool. I'm afraid you've dialled the wrong number! Goodbye."

He put his mobile phone back in his pocket. Jennie was looking at him questioningly.

"Well, it was just a..."

"... Somebody who dialled the wrong number! I heard that."

"I know you did!"

"And... What are we supposed to be doing?"

He hesitated for a second, visibly troubled.

"Oh, we were about to have a romantic kiss, weren't we?"

He came close to Jennie to take her in his arms again, but she pushed him back gently.

"What's wrong, Gary? Is it that woman on the phone?"

"It's just her voice, you know", he answered, having found nothing else.

"What about her voice?"

"It's just as if I had heard it before, but..."

"... But...?"

"Never mind. Let's forget about it. It doesn't matter, after all, does it?"

"I guess it doesn't."

"I think I'd better switch that bloody phone off, anyway."

"You can't do that!"

"Why?"

"You just can't switch that bloody phone off!

What if Beverley or Bobby had an accident or something? How would your parents join us? They don't even know which hotel we're staying at."

"You're right, love. You're perfectly right. I won't switch it off. Shall we have a kiss now?"

"Let's have a romantic kiss!"

The weather was still fine on Friday afternoon. They had visited Newport Roman Villa in the morning, had lunch at the Blacksmiths Arms and phoned the children. Gary had kept his fingers crossed since the evening before and hoped that Martha wouldn't call him again.

"I like it", Jennie declared, "although I'm not sure Charles I did."

"Nobody's been beheaded here for quite a long time. Let's go in", he answered, showing the entrance of Carisbrooke Castle Museum.

After the visit, they went to the shop and found a guide to the castle for Gary's father.

"He will like it. As for mum... Oh look, beautiful box, isn't it, love?"

"You shouldn't, Gary. You know how greedy she can be. Toffees are not good for her health."

"She loves them!"

"Well, if you want to kill your mother!"

"She must have eaten thousands of toffees in her life! A few more won't kill her!"

"It's up to you."

"Well, the replica of Osborne House you bought yesterday is all right for your mum, but what will you buy for your dad?"

She hesitated a few seconds.

"What about toffees?" she answered

mischievously, "he's always been overweight, what change will it make?"

"Excellent idea! What about the children?"

"We'll find something for them at Bembridge tomorrow morning."

"O.K. Shall we have a walk on the beach first? And go shopping afterwards?"

"It sounds great to me. Let's go now. I'm looking forward to a nice meal tonight."

"So am I."

As a matter of fact, they went shopping first on the morrow, then they went to the beach and had a picnic there before leaving Bembridge Coast Hotel. They took the ferry at half past one for the return crossing. They fetched Bobby and Beverley at Gary's parents', had dinner there and went back home by nine.

On Monday morning, after greeting his colleagues, Gary had a look in his pigeonhole. He found nothing new but an envelope. He knew at once it was from Martha, who had been clever enough not to call him again, knowing that he would hang up on her if Jennie happened to be around. He read it with attention and anxiety.

Martha Spencer
28 Liddon Road
BR1 Bromley

Friday, October 30th

Dear Gary,

Since I saw you again, I've been thinking of all the good times we once had together. When I look at Sarah's face, it's as if I could see yours. She and Beverley look quite alike, don't they? I think Bobby takes after his mother. A beautiful woman, actually; she was the only one in the family I didn't know. You certainly love her, but you must remember how much you loved me. I'm sure you still do. Harry is a nice guy, I must admit, and I like him a lot. I do appreciate him, but I still love you. Let's revive our old affair, so let's have dinner together at 'Con Amore', an Italian restaurant, on Thursday night. You generally practise aikido from eight to ten, don't you? Jennie won't expect to see you back before half past ten, maybe eleven. So, if we meet by seven, we'll have plenty of time, for dinner first and, if we have an affinity, as we obviously do, for rediscovering each other.

Needless to say that you can't refuse my proposal. As you said, you have your family and I have mine. It would be such a great pity to upset them. Of course, none of them will ever know about our relation.

See you on Thursday night.

With all my love,

Martha

Unfortunately for Gary, the content of Martha's letter confirmed his fears. She was a kind of lunatic who would make a mess of his life if he let her blackmail him, which he didn't intend to do although he was aware that he was trapped, that his freedom of action had narrowed. What if he went to the restaurant and tried to explain to her that he would never satisfy her request, not to say her demand? It would be useless for she wouldn't listen to him. She wouldn't leave him alone and would try to call him any time; she might even wait for him outside the school or speak to Jenny and tell her they had a love affair or, worst of all, tell Bobby and Beverley about their half-sister. What if he just ignored her invitation? The consequence would be the same; it might be even worse as she would feel outraged.

All day long, he was preoccupied with this awkward matter. He thought about telling Jennie, but how could he do that? When they had met Martha at the shopping centre, he had introduced her as 'Mrs Spencer', the woman he had had an appointment with the week before the holidays. How could he say, now, 'well, love, you know, that Mrs Spencer we met the other day, do you remember? Well, she happens to be my former girlfriend, the one I was with before I met you'? Furthermore, it wouldn't be easy to add, with a smile, 'by the way, you should know that I'm her daughter's father... Sarah, the one I teach... As a result, I have three children, but you don't have to worry. Everything's under control!'

At lunch-time, Jarvis Wester, a history teacher he

was friend with, asked him if he was feeling well.

"Are you all right, Gary?"

"I'm fine, Jarvis. I'm just thinking."

"Just thinking, uh? Rather dismal kind of thoughts, I'm afraid."

He changed the subject, but he didn't fool her.

"Well, if you feel like speaking about your problem..."

He burst out laughing.

"I didn't mean to say anything funny, but..."

"... It's just that, you know, they always say that in movies, so... Let's talk about something else, anyway."

"As you wish! But, seriously, if..."

"Please, Jarvis, don't!'

The afternoon was long and awful. When he left the school, unhappy and exhausted, he had finally made up his mind to speak to Jennie and show her the letter. If he hadn't been able to hide his confusion from Jarvis, how on earth could he hide it from his wife? Whatever Jennie's reaction might be, and he feared it indeed, he had come to the conclusion that it was the only thing and, above all, the best thing to do, for whatever she was to learn about that 'old affair', she had to learn it from him.

It was raining over High Street. Martha was wearing a long raincoat and a silk scarf along with a tartan umbrella. She had to use both her hands to hold it because of the abrupt changes of the wind. As she was approaching the restaurant, she noticed a stout young man walking hurriedly towards her, struggling as she was to control an oversized black umbrella. Although she tilted hers away from his, she couldn't avoid the smash. The man mumbled a few words of apology and continued on his way, quickening his pace.

It was twenty past seven by her watch when she reached 'Con Amore'. She was early. She folded her umbrella and stepped into the restaurant. The waiter greeted her with a cheerful 'good evening, madam'.

"Good evening, I'm Mrs Spencer."

"Glad to meet you, Mrs Spencer. A table for two, isn't it?"

"That's it."

"This way, please."

He nodded towards a table.

"Shall I take your coat, please?"

She found his Italian accent pleasant. She handed her raincoat and her scarf to him. She was attractive in her black dress with a plunging neckline. She sat and began to read the menu to kill time. She wondered if she would take two courses or three, and decided that two would be enough for both Gary and her, then they would have plenty of time left after dinner. She was thrilled at the idea of seeing him enter the restaurant and give himself up to her. She would play with him like a cat with its prey. A very good friend of hers, a businesswoman who was often away from London during the week, had given her the keys of her flat which was located in Church Road, a few minutes from High Street. She would take him there and he would be hers again.

She examined the starters thoroughly, hesitating between 'zuppa del giorno', a name she liked because it was easy to understand, and 'avocado al forno'. The 'soup of the day' would be very welcome as the weather was wet and cold, but the 'baked avocado with prawns and cheese topping' was tempting. As a main course, the 'breast of duck with black cherries sauce' found favour with her although she had nothing against 'salmon with leeks and white wine'. The dinner promised to be a real treat. 'Unforgettable!' she thought.

"Good evening, Mrs Spencer!" a lady standing in front of her said.

Martha couldn't believe her eyes. The restaurant was almost empty. Apart from a couple at the other end of the room, the waiter and two waitresses, they were alone, looking into each other's eyes.

"May I have a seat?"

The atmosphere had become tense. Martha didn't answer.

"Gary will not come, so I guess this chair is free. I hope you don't mind."

Jennie sat down. "We have to talk", she said, "let me tell you a story. As you may know, I'm a midwife..."

Martha looked surprised.

"... Don't you? You seem to know so many things about my husband and my children! Well, I see you've neglected me a little bit, but it doesn't matter. Let me come back to my story; maybe I should say 'our' story... When I met Gary, you and he had just broken up..."

"Will you have a drink before dinner?" the waiter interrupted.

"Two glasses of white wine, please", Jennie answered, "... I worked, and I still do, at the Princess Royal University Hospital, where you gave birth to Sarah. When you came for a prenatal visit in May, I was there. You didn't pay attention to me but I knew who you were and I was intrigued when I learnt that your baby was due in August. We met again in July for your last visit; I wasn't there the day when you had your baby. A full-term delivery! I hardly need to point out that I had easily concluded that Sarah had been conceived in November, which meant that Gary could be her father. It was only a possibility, of course, but from the bottom of my heart, I knew he was. I never told him about Sarah, until Monday night, when he showed me your letter. He was feeling so uneasy! Yet he was honest with me and I'm most grateful to him for confiding in me. When we met at the Glades Shopping Centre, I recognized you at once and I had a sense of impending danger. I saw it on Gary's face. When your daughter's name slipped out of my mouth after our encounter, he was amazed. On Monday, I told him that I had met you at the maternity ward. You see, we are a united couple and there is no room for you, or anyone else, between us. Checkmate! Game is over! Don't feel obliged, to take your revenge, to let our children know that they have a half-sister;

Gary and I will protect them against your malice if we have to. But, above all, even if your husband is perfectly aware that Sarah isn't his biological daughter, I think there's no need to twist the knife in the wound, and just think how harmful it would be for her. Please leave us alone, and don't victimize Sarah; she doesn't deserve it."

Martha was on the verge of tears. She tried to speak, but she couldn't. She was stunned. "I'm so ashamed", she finally managed to say in a tearful voice.

Jennie had first intended to conclude her monologue with a scathing 'have a nice meal!' but Martha had humiliated herself enough. The anger she had felt had turned into pity. She stood up slowly, said goodbye and went to the counter. She paid for the two glasses of wine and left 'Con Amore'.